VIRGINIA HAMILTON

Second Cousins

SCHOLASTIC
Signature

an imprint of
Scholastic Inc.

New York · Toronto · London · Auckland · Sydney
Mexico City · New Delhi · Hong Kong

This book was originally published in hardcover by
The Blue Sky Press in 1998.

The fractal images in this book were produced by
Virginia Hamilton, using 1997 Cygnus Software, Fractal eXtreme.

Please visit Virginia Hamilton on her
Web site at: www.virginiahamilton.com.

Book design by Kathleen Westray

ISBN 0-590-47369-7

12 11 10 9 8 7 6 5   2 3 4 5/0

Printed in the U.S.A   40

First Scholastic Trade paperback printing, February 2000

TO "ALL US,"
THE FAMILY

CHAPTER ONE

Dog Days

❧

CAMMY COLEMAN pedaled her dirt bike as fast as it would go. She pulled her cousin, Elodie, behind her. Elodie clung to the lock chain and skated dangerously fast on one in-line skate.

"Too ill!" Elodie shouted.

"Way cool, El!" Cammy hollered as they sped down the street.

Their skate-bike game was this summer's favorite. They were practically flying; they both loved speed, and daring danger. They were third cousins, and both were twelve.

"Don't you dare slow down!" Elodie yelled. "This is fu-u-un!"

"It's fun, all right. I'll hit a bump, and then we'll see how fun it is." *Crash! But that's way whac,*

Cammy thought. *If you think fear, you'll crash for sure.* "Are you ready?"

"Not yet, Cam! Let me glide some. And don't slow until I let go!" Elodie hollered high and loud, which was the way her voice got when she was having fun. She had a sure grip on the bike chain. "Ooh! I'm gonna be famous!"

"So crazy!" Cammy muttered. Always talking about becoming famous. *El, you don't tell me what to do! So country, and bold, you skinny thing!* Cammy didn't want to be mean. But just last year, Elodie had been a half-hungry crop-picker.

Cammy never said a word. She kept on going fast down the street.

Things had changed since that dark time of Cammy's first cousin — Patricia Ann. A whole summer ago, it was. Last August. Her aunt Effie's perfect daughter. Just awful — "Drowned, and gone to heaven," was what people said.

All the day-camp kids from last summer were different because of Patty Ann. Cammy saw some of them at the town pool, where she and Elodie spent these hot summer days. Day camp was for younger kids. That made Cammy smile. Younger was what she, Elodie, and Patty Ann had been last year.

Patty Ann would never be a year older.

Why am I thinking about her now? Cammy wondered. *Can't help it. We're bigger, me 'n' El; a whole year older,* she thought. *Subtract Patty Ann from who she was — my cousin.*

"One from one leaves . . . no one," she'd told Elodie. "Leaves a zero. But there's still us two, alive; and we've been through a lot."

She didn't like to be reminded of last summer. Every day-camp kid, clinging to the bank of the swollen Little River, saw Patty Ann save Elodie and then drown, herself. Every kid, especially Cammy and Elodie, had been scarred by the tragedy.

For a long time after, all-them had this awful kind of hurt look, like it was their fault. They noticed it about each other. And all year, it seemed like they had to make their way through an aching dark to get to a peaceful day time. That's how Cammy saw it all. They had to go on with what they had to keep looking through. It changed them.

A look, a cold flash of regret, hurt. *Oh, stop it!*

"Now!" Elodie hollered.

At once, Cammy was back in the game. She pedaled furiously, holding the bike as straight as she could. At the exact moment she felt was right, she put on the brakes as hard as she dared.

Hold tight! Don't get pitched over the handlebars!

Letting go of her hold on the chain, Elodie whipped out from behind Cammy. In a second, she was out in front and speeding off down the street.

Cammy sat there on her bike, watching, as El spread her arms. El slanted forward with her left leg extended behind her as she leaned into a long, beautiful glide on the right skate.

"Wow!" Cammy said. "Too ill, El. Great trick! That's a ten, almost."

"What *almost*!" Elodie practically screamed.

Cammy smiled, admiring El's long glide. "I bet you've gone a *hunnert* feet!"

"And still going! Stil-l-l-ll going! El, the Famous! Yonk, yonk, yonk!" Elodie screeched, holding the pose. Then, she wobbled. "Oooh! I forget — Cammeeeey!"

"Crouch, bend your knees! Lift your toe-front! No! Just easy, El!" Cammy hollered at her. "The brake has to touch the ground — stop you!" El had forgotten how to use the brake, or where it was. "El? The back of your skate!" That was where the brake was.

But it wasn't easy on one skate. The trick was to keep the left foot up out of the action and keep your body balanced on the right skate. *Sure to crack an anklebone if you do let the left foot down while going so fast,* Cammy thought.

They hadn't skated since the pool opened, they'd been so busy swimming.

"Oooh!" Elodie moaned. Still going fast, she bent her knee. "Yeah." The skate heel with the brake hit the ground. She kept her arms outstretched.

"That's it, El!" Cammy called, and started after her. Suddenly, Elodie slanted to the right. At the same moment, her skate made a sliding sound in the loose dirt and small stones near the curbside. She went down, hitting the pavement and stones with her hands out, and on her knees. Then, she was rolling over, one knee at a time.

It happened so fast. She'd braked, all right. But too speedy, too near the gravelly curb.

So sudden, it took Cammy's breath. A hard fall.

The next thing, Elodie was on her side, holding one knee with both hands. Cammy was there in a second. She let the bike crash to the pavement.

"Ow, oooh! Ow-ow!" El's eyes were squeezed shut; she screwed up her face in pain.

"Aw, El!" Cammy rushed over to her. She felt cold inside. And scared to death. "Are you hurt?" *Well, duh! Hope to goodness she didn't break something.* "L-O-D?" Cammy said, trying to make light. "Are you okay?"

She knew El wasn't, as she kneeled next to her.

A car horn blew at them. "Oh, man!" Cammy had dropped her bike right in the middle of the street. Didn't even realize. "Sorry!" Embarrassed, Cammy went back and pulled her bike to the side.

"Shouldn't be playing in the street!" the woman driver shouted, and drove on.

Who asked you? Cammy thought. "Well, duh!

Wonder whose mama she thinks she is?" Cammy said. "Do you know her?"

"Nuh-uh," Elodie answered. "If I hadn't been hurt, I'da skitched her!"

"Cool!" Cammy smiled. She could just see El hanging on to the back of the car on one skate, hitching a ride at car speed. That was skitching.

But it wouldn't do if Cammy's mom, Maylene, heard about the game they'd been playing in the street.

"Oooh," Elodie moaned.

"Take your hand away so I can see," Cammy said, although she really didn't want to look at some bad wound.

She kneeled close, hoping she wouldn't have to see Elodie's knee bone. *Eh-ew!* What would it look like?

"It hurts!" Elodie cried. Her eyes brimmed with tears.

"Let go of it, El. Let me put your towel around it."

Elodie let go, and the blood came. Her hand was full of red. There was a long scrape on her knee. The broken skin was peeled back. Ugly-looking.

"Don't touch it!" Elodie said. "Oooh. Ahhhh! It hurts sooo bad!"

Cammy watched a big ball of blood boil out of the pale flesh. She shivered, she couldn't help it. She shivered again and swallowed.

"I know it hurts you bad. Let me just wipe it," Cammy told Elodie. "Shoot! It's got dirt in it!"

"Ohhhh, ooooh." Elodie started to shake as Cammy eased the towel from around her neck. "My hands hurt. My wrists . . ."

"See, I'll just put the very end down to soak up the blood," Cammy said.

"Let me do it," Elodie whined. She took the towel and pressed it on the scrape. "Oooh-ow-ow . . . Why come we don't have some water?"

"Well, we just don't," Cammy said. She hadn't remembered to bring it. And they hadn't taken the time for knee pads or wrist braces, either, even though Cammy had them. They should have.

"They say if you press down hard, it'll stop bleeding," Cammy said.

"Well, I'm trying to!" Pitiful sounding. "You don't know how bad it hurts!" Elodie began to cry.

"I know it hurts," Cammy said kindly. "Ole Cool-El!"

Sobbing, El leaned her head against Cammy's.

They sat there a while, shoulder to shoulder, by the side of the road. Cammy stared at the dirt bike her dad had given her for Christmas. She owned it, so it was her job to bring some water. *Should've taken the time to get out the knee pads and wrist braces, too,* she thought. It was her responsibility.

Soon, Elodie felt better. Her crying changed to short gasps, then deep breaths and long sighs. She still held the towel to her knee. Took a dry end of it to wipe her eyes.

Cammy examined El's hands. They were scraped, but not bleeding. She told El to bend her wrist; no broken bones.

"You know, the 'union is in two days," Cammy thought to say, to make her cousin feel better.

"Ooooh, yeah!" El exclaimed, remembering. "The 'union is this weekend!" Elodie sat up straighter, and grinned.

Another car went by. And another. Cammy and Elodie pretended they were resting, talking. They'd moved over to sit on the curb. Cammy now had both skates around her neck. Elodie had one shoe on.

"It's hot when you're not riding," Cammy said, hoping to keep El's mind away from her hurt.

"I know it," El answered, shakily.

"The dog days of August are just the stillest. And the best hottest ninety degrees of all summer," Cammy said.

"Word . . ." Elodie's voice was hushed, still with pain in it.

They were sweating, and breathing strong, like they'd been running. But they were coming down some. They breathed the same, *like sisters*, Cammy thought, again.

She only had one brother — Andrew. Elodie had brothers, but they were much older. Some-time pickers with their families. Just like Elodie's mom was, all summer long, way north and way south. Elodie said the families each could make ten thousand a year. But usually, they made six or seven. They knew they were poor. The brothers wanted better jobs. But her mom liked it the way it was.

El's mom, Marie Lewis Odie, would find her way back to El around the end of September. Greeting Cammy's mom, Maylene, she'd probably say what she usually said — "It's a living. It's steady every season. I do love breathin' in the out-of-the-doors."

"Your mom will come here soon," Cammy thought to say.

"'Cause the 'union is on Saturday!"

"Let's don't talk about it," Cammy said. Today was Thursday. "Or it'll never come."

"Right," El said. "I won't talk about it."

"Glad you are here with us, though, and going to school with me," is the way Cammy had put it to El one time. And Elodie, becoming shy with her, smiling down at her hands, said Cammy and her mom were neat for taking her in.

Made Cammy proud to help her, too. Now, sitting by her wounded cousin in the heat of late lunchtime, Cammy was glad to have El with her every day.

"We're older this year, the two of us," Cammy said. A serious look passed between them.

"I know it," El said. She sat up straighter. The

knee pain seemed to be less as she let out shaky breaths.

Elodie's blood had seeped through the towel. They watched, but it didn't spread. Gently, Elodie lifted the towel and peeked at her knee. "Oooh! It looks sooo bad!"

"But, see, it's crusting, I think," Cammy said. "You want to get on home now?"

"Yeah. I hurt. Get my shoe for me?"

Cammy got Elodie's shoe out of the bike basket. Her shoes were sneakers, just like Cammy's.

Carefully Cammy slipped the sneaker on Elodie's foot.

Last year, after the drowning, it seemed the whole world hated Elodie for having been saved. Kids got crazy and said the ghost of Patty Ann was in El. Got so bad, she had to leave town and go stay with her mom, picking apples. Back then, Cammy's mom had said, "If I could take her in, I would." And her mom was as good as her word. Just before Thanksgiving, El came to live with them. But it was Cammy's dad who'd bought the bunk beds and new dressers for them both. A desk they shared. A small TV.

I could live with my dad, I guess. Me and El both, Cammy thought now.

All so much had happened since Patty Ann's death. Cammy's dad had his business. But he'd moved closer, from another town to a big old place a few miles out, where all the farms began. Sometimes, Andrew and their cousin, Richie, stayed out there on weekends. Richie was Aunt Effie's son.

But why should I live there? Cammy wondered. *I like where I am with my mom and Andrew.*

Her dad was way cool, though. He might not live in the same house, but he gave a lot of extras to help out with El.

Elodie really didn't cost much extra, Maylene said. Cammy's dad gave extra for special things, such as her bike. Still, Maylene was the best.

"Your mom is just way prime, taking me in," El had said.

There was something about a mom with you every morning and every night, to care for you. But then there was Aunt Effie. She was over to their house almost all day.

Talking about Aunt Effie, Maylene told them, "She has this absence in her heart. Cammy, both you and Elodie be nice to her." Effie was her mom's big sister and Cammy's aunt. Aunt Effie's daughter was Cammy's drowned cousin, Patty Ann.

Almost a whole year had gone by since the bad time of last August and the drowning. "She's gotten a lot better," her mom said about Effie.

Cammy could tell her mom something, in answer to that.

CHAPTER TWO

750

It didn't take them long to get there. Home wasn't huge, like new houses on other streets, but it wasn't too small. Theirs was an older part of town.

Home was on a side street off a bigger, noisier one. It had a front yard with a flower bed and a side yard with a big shade tree. All of it, the yards, the house, was 750 Massy Street. Once, it had been called Massy Creek Road when there were mostly farms and not many houses. But now it was a street much like any other in town, and it had sidewalks all up and down. Her mom said the town put the sidewalks in when Cammy was very young, around the time her mom and dad started going different directions.

Cammy couldn't remember missing her dad over

the years. "Out of sight, out of mind," Andrew said. Her dad had lived in another town then. But she must've missed him some way. And then, last August, she had gotten to know him. She'd been practically out of her mind over her drowned cousin, and her dad had come and stayed close to her. There with Andrew, him, all the time coming over while her mom was at work. In one way, last August seemed like years ago. In another way, it was like every day, always in her head.

Her mom said the last time Cammy had seen all of her cousins was when she was six. Second, and even third and fourth cousins had come from way faraway places. Cammy thought of them all as second cousins she'd seen but couldn't remember.

"Seems like I recall a big party," she was telling El now, on the way home.

"Was I in it?" Elodie wanted to know.

"Well, as if . . . !" Cammy exclaimed. But then she thought about it. "I was way too little to remember anything. And you must've been, too. If you were there. And I'm not saying you were, either."

"Oh, yeah," Elodie said. She looked like she really wanted to have been at that party.

"But so what?" Cammy said. "We're together now. And you're my real third cousin. 'Cause your mom is my mom's second cousin. See?"

"That's right," Elodie said, none too happily.

"I've got lots of second cousins," Cammy said.

"Then so do I!" Elodie exclaimed.

Cammy didn't argue it. "Well," she said, "we'll just tell everybody you're a second cousin, too. Okay?"

"O-okay!"

"We'll see all our cousins at the 'union — don't talk about it!" Cammy said. They were home, wheeling up the short driveway to the side of the house.

"Promise you'll help clean up my knee before anybody sees us," Elodie said. "They'll figure out I didn't have the knee pads on."

"Right," Cammy said.

They had to sneak in the house past whomever was there and into the bathroom upstairs. Aunt Effie was usually visiting. And likely she was in the new room they'd built for Gram Tut, made from the alcove at the end of the dining room.

They did it fast. Once upstairs, Cammy soaked a towel in warm water and gently cleaned Elodie's wound. Elodie screwed up her face in the worst ugly grimace she could make.

"Don't put me on, El."

"I ain't! It hurts bad!"

"Okay, finished. Now quiet! I'll put on some Band-Aids."

Downstairs, she could hear Aunt Effie. "Cammy? Cam!"

"Coming!" Cammy called to Aunt Effie.

Silence. Well. Aunt Effie was a real pill. There was

always something, gray clouds and rain, about her. But they managed to stand her.

Quickly, Cammy and Elodie changed into dry T-shirts and grabbed clean towels, to take back to the pool. Cammy led the way down the stairs. They left their towels at the bottom, to pick up later when they went out again. They crept through the dining room to the new room. They were careful not to make noise.

Aunt Effie was leaning over Gram Tut's bed as they came in. She was muttering something and fluffing the pillows beneath Tut, who was sleeping. Effie was dressed in her usual black smock and black housedress. Black stockings and black shoes. Andrew said Aunt Effie looked like a nightmare in a thunderstorm. She did always seem to be anger's weather.

Effie turned at the slight sound of Cammy and Elodie. She did not greet them, but moved away to sit in her chair by the bed. Aunt Effie didn't have to tell them what to do. They walked right up to her and stood there, looking at the floor.

"Can't speak to somebody?" Aunt Effie muttered.

"Hello, Aunt Effie," Cammy said. *Duh!* Sometimes, like today, they forgot to greet her first, the way she liked.

"'H'lo, An' Effie," Elodie managed.

Effie grabbed both of them, none too gently. They had to look her full in her face. She put a hand on each one's shoulder, and closed her eyes. They could feel her dry hands through their T-shirts.

Elodie squeezed her eyes shut, but Cammy wouldn't. She watched Aunt Effie's face and wondered what her aunt was saying to herself.

"Forgive them, for they are bad children!" was what Andrew had guessed.

Her mom said Effie really didn't mean any harm.

Then why did Aunt Effie lay her hands on them every day? "It really upsets El," Cammy told her mom. It upset Cammy, too. But she could hide it. El just couldn't take it at all.

"Effie thinks you owe it to her," Maylene had told her. "Let her have her way. It makes it easier for her — no girl of her own anymore."

Now Cammy put her arm around Elodie, careful not to touch Aunt Effie's hand on El's shoulder. She could feel the tiny tremors that had started through El's bony back. She felt them grow bigger, like ripples on water, widening. Then El began to shudder; and still Aunt Effie had her eyes closed, probably saying all kinds of mean things about them to herself.

I hate this every day. I can't stand it today, Cammy thought. *You keep trying to blame El and me. El, mostly, because Patty Ann saved her, and then drowned herself. Just you stop it!* But Aunt Effie kept on. El's nerves were going to jump out of her skin, Cammy knew.

Angrily, Cammy said, "Just quit it!" She couldn't take it anymore. She jerked herself and El free. "I know all about you!" She didn't care what Aunt Effie thought of her, either.

Effie's eyes shot open; she stared at Cammy. Made Cammy feel like some little animal on a dark road, blinded by headlights. *I know something,* Cammy thought. *Aunt Effie, you are as crazy as you were after Patty Ann drowned. I was sick from it, too, but I got better. You never did.*

Suddenly, Effie stood up. She glanced at the bed once. Then, not looking at either Cammy or Elodie, she stalked out of the room.

"Well ex-cu-u-se me!" Elodie mumbled. She took a deep breath, glad Aunt Effie's grasp had been broken. "She is way scary! I hate her!"

"Shhh," Cammy said. She felt she should be quiet in this place that was her good Gram's bedroom.

Having Gram Tut out of the Care Center and home filled Cammy with delight. Knew she felt all the love she could for her Gram and knew she always would. She had warned El to whisper. And now they spoke not a word out loud as they came up close to the bed together.

Cammy sat down and ran her fingers through the softest, most cottony hair she'd ever felt. Fanned out on the pillowcase, it had turned yellowish from age. And there was Gram Tut's little wrinkly face in the middle of the hair-fan. Cammy's good grandmom.

Something about her grandmom made Cammy's days just so full of delight. Cammy's Gram Tut, who was Maylene and Aunt Effie's mother. Big as life! But so small, tiny there in her bed. Gram was as sweet as could be.

"She's so way old, why'd they let her out of that Care place she lived in?" Elodie had asked one day. Like it was something bad to be old as Gram, and in, then out, of the Care Center.

"Because she's got family here, and she's well enough to come home," Cammy had told her. "We make her feel better. She can go back, if she gets real bad," Cammy had said. "Don't talk like that about my Gram!"

Andrew said that when Gram came to live with them, Elodie had been afraid they'd send her away. "Gram Tut looks like a dried prune," El had said. "Her teeth come out; An' Effie puts-um in a glass. Can't she put-um in a drawer, somethin'?"

"You just shut up about my Gram!" Cammy had said, and told her mom.

"You want to stay here?" Maylene asked Elodie. "Don't ever speak ill of Mom Tut. She's the most cherished part of us. And she gives Effie something more to think about than her dead child."

Put El straight. Made her careful what she said out loud.

CHAPTER THREE

Tut

❧

SOMETHING IN HER HAIR, moving around. It wasn't buzzing, but it still might could be hornets. She'd found a whole hornet's nest up in the white lilac one time. She'd had Emmet take a flame on a stick up there and burn them out. He'd done himself up in mosquito nets. Gracious. That was supposed to keep him from getting stung! Oh, she'd laughed so hard at him!

But he did it. Set the hive afire and swung down from a mid-high branch before the hornets knew what had hit them. Sweet-smelling scent of lilacs all in his hair. Emmet and she had run inside the house. When they'd gone back to see, there was nothing left of the nest but fine, black paper — what the nest looked like after the fire.

The dream turned. Tut saw babies. Cute! All over the place, crawling in the snow. Just had their diapers on — no clothes! They were hunting Easter eggs. It made sense to her. Dreaming, she fried two eggs in a skillet in her kitchen, talking the whole time to baby Maylene in her high chair. Maylene, sweet child! Followed Tut's every move with her sweet brown eyes. "Mommmmma!" she called, "MMMMMMMMMMMMMMommmma!" working her mouth over her favorite sound, and sucking warm toast spread with honey. That child! Apple of Emmet's eye. S'why he often called her Baby D., for Delicious. Well, as time passed, they'd shortened Tut's real name, Tutwilla, to Tut, so Baby D. Maylene could say it. And it was Tut, or Mom, Mom Tut.

Tut felt the hand on her hair. Now she knew what it was. She was waking, quietly, knowing she had dreams but not knowing what they were about. She sensed children near.

She woke up, talking. "Stay out of the sunhot. Help me with these cukes. Get all the black soil off of them. Then, we need to shine them. Emmet's taking them to town market."

"Hi, Gram," Cammy said brightly. "You're dreaming again!"

Tut's eyes fluttered a moment, then opened. "Where am I?" She looked around. "What is this place?"

"Now, Gram," Cammy said. She smoothed Tut's hair back from her forehead. "Got a kiss for you. Mmmm! Don't wash it off, but let it grow!"

"Where am I?" Tut asked again.

"You're home, here with my mom, Maylene, and me, and L-O-D!" She smiled at her gram. "Oh, and Aunt Effie, too — she comes over, takes good care of you." *Well, duh!*

"I don't know — ! My Maylene is just a . . . I want to go home!" Tut's eyes filled with tears.

Cammy held her Gram's hand. Rolled her face gently on Tut's shoulder. "Don't be sad! Gram! It's me and El right here with you. We come to see you. You want us to go away?"

Now Gram had her hand in Cammy's hair. She reached out with her other hand. Elodie knew what to do. Reluctantly, she came around the other side of the bed. Knew she had to. A look from Cammy told her so.

Gram Tut held El as close as she did Cammy. Felt her hair.

"Bad, both of you. Hair all damp!" Gram said, sounding more awake and like herself. "Where have you all been?"

"We been swimming, Gram," Cammy said.

"We *have* been swimming!" Tut said. Then, this: "Now, you watch that crick when it rains, because the water will rise fastest and become a river. Don't go near after a rain."

"Gram, we have a pool," Cammy said. "The town built us kids a pool! Remember? I told you about it."

Tut looked Cammy full in the face. "Oh, yes, now I remember. Well. Don't play too hard."

Cammy smiled at her. "You always tell us that, Gram."

Tut rested further into her pillow. Closed her eyes.

The crick was high. Emmet had her on his shoulders. She carried Baby D., cradled in her arms. Emmet had the bawling Effie in a sling, tied over one shoulder and under the other. Baby D. slept through the whole crossing of the crick. It only took about thirty minutes. Emmet held on to Tut by her knees; her skirts were wrapped tightly around her legs.

Tut prayed that a wave of water wouldn't come suddenly down the hillside to wash precious Baby D. clean from her. How came a little crick to grow so wide and high! April storm, and crick water was cold from late snow, melted.

By the time Emmet got them out of there, his legs and arms were about frozen. He nearly dropped her and Baby D. Nearly caught a bad current, would carry them to danger. But Emmet was strong. Yet he slipped backward and fell halfway down in the icy water before he righted himself. Got poor little Effie all wet. Effie had held her breath. Later, Emmet nearly lost his toes from frostbite. Effie screamed all night.

"She's breathin' too hard," El said softly. "She's moaning about something. She hurting?" she asked Cammy.

Cammy shook her head. "Gram, you want to get up?" *No,* she thought. *Better wait for Aunt Effie or Mom.* She wondered if Aunt Effie bothered Gram somehow. Cammy thought of something. "Gram! Guess what? The 'union's coming at the end of the week! Won't that be fun? I haven't seen those cousins of mine since I was six."

"I've never seen them!" El piped up.

"Gram! It's the 'union, you know? And I can't even remember."

After a moment, Gram breathed deeply. Eyes wide open on the ceiling. "Was a long time," she said. "Long time ago. Told." Gone-time of the great-grands. Yes. The soldiers, of the Union, led all-them clear to here.

"Even after they was partly safe. Told, it was. They crossed the big water . . . still had to cross that crick." Tut mumbled the words.

Cammy could make out only part of it. "Gram, what crick are you talking about? I want to know."

* * *

Well. Had a deep hole in it, that crick. Tut, seeing it all clearly in her mind. Water, high — seems to me a young girl drowned there just now. . . . You wouldn't know that hole water was sucking at you until too late. You'd fall down in it and not be seen again. Now, 'course, Emmet knew to take care. Some did fall, too; told, in the gone-time. Always, we hold to the Union along that crick crossing.

"Gram?"

"Oh, hush!" Tut told Cammy. "Get me up from here, I want to go to see my baby. . . ."

Elodie giggled. "Your baby is big as she can be," Cammy said.

"Don't think I know my Maylene? I know how big she is," Tut said.

Tut tried to get out of bed, just as Andrew came through the door. "Well, I'll be," he said. "Gram, what's going on? What's up wit you?"

Tut grinned. "Don't say wit," she said, but not unkindly. She did so admire Andrew, a slim, younger image of Maylene and Tut's own Emmet. He had Emmet's shoulders, Maylene's long legs. "Don't you children learn anything in that school?"

"Now, Grammy Tut-tut," Andrew said.

"Don't call me names!" Tut said. And the three of them laughed at her. She didn't mind. "Get me up!" she demanded.

"Okay, okay," Andrew told her. "Just wait a tired minute."

He went out of the room. "Hey, Aunt Effie, Tut-tut wants to get up." They could hear Effie from the kitchen.

"She already was just up, and ate," Effie said. "She don't remember a thing anymore!"

"Well, she wants up again."

"Maybe she's hungry some more," Cammy said.

And then, Gram piped up. "I want to sit and eat with the children."

"You know what time it is, don't you, Gram?" Cammy asked.

"Lunchtime!" Elodie said.

Aunt Effie came in. She did not look at Cammy or Elodie. She reluctantly gave Andrew a look and a nod. "Can't speak to somebody?"

"Aunt Effie, you're here every day, and so am I. So, hi — and that's enough. We don't have to be so formal."

"You're here early," she said, grudgingly.

"Checking on Cammy and El."

"That's my job," Effie told him.

"Mom says they're about big enough to take care of themselves. Mom says your job is to take care of Gram. You don't have any children to worry about. Richie maybe, but he's no child."

Well, it shocked Cammy. But she could tell that Andrew had spoken before he thought. It just slipped out. He hadn't been thinking about Patty Ann.

At his words, Aunt Effie seemed to draw herself in. Looked dark as a storm in her face. Her eyes fluttered, staring all around her, as if she saw what they couldn't see. She smiled, and nodded to herself, just crazy. But then, suddenly, she turned calmly away from them. "You all, get out!" she said. A second later she asked, "Mom? You want up?" Spoken in a kind and friendly voice to her mother.

Gram Tut gave a soft sound, not quite a laugh, not a sigh. "Yes, Effie, please. Sit in the kitchen with the children."

"Well, then, we'll get you up," Effie said. "Put your slippers and your robe on over the house gown."

"She's wacko!" Elodie whispered about Effie as they entered the kitchen.

"Don't say that," Andrew told her. "She might hear you. Look, see, she's not so crazy that she doesn't fix lunch for you all. Nice sandwiches. Lemonade. Chips."

"Probably poison," Cammy couldn't help saying.

"Now quit it!" Andrew said. "You eat and then go back to the pool. Rest for a half hour before you go in again."

"Gram Tut wants to see us!" Cammy said.

"After she sees you, get out of Aunt Effie's way. She's in a mood."

"Du-uh? For days," Cammy said.

Andrew shot her a look but didn't say anything.

Aunt Effie was leading Gram Tut in. "She wants to walk some," Effie said. Usually, Gram went around in her wheelchair.

"I want to walk," Tut said, leaning on Effie, then standing and resting.

Emmet, Tut was thinking. We'd walk in the gorges. Didn't mind them. We'd stay out all day, peel sassafras bark for tea, and pick spicebush berries for seasoning. We'd sit with our feet dangling in the crick. And fall asleep in the sun. We'd come back to that place, so hidden on the side of the cliff, what with all the tall shrubs and black walnut — you wouldn't never notice it if you passed our way. Oh it was grand, when Emmet lived, and walked with me.

And will be again. She heard him speak to her so clearly. Gram smiled, and with tiny, shuffling steps, she walked to the kitchen.

"Sit, Gram!" Cammy said, seeing her so happy. Gram was helped into the chair at the head of the kitchen table.

"Blessings on these," Aunt Effie said.

"Blessed be," they murmured back.

Effie gave soup to Gram. "Anybody want some?" It was vegetable and looked good. The girls nodded. "Andrew?" she asked.

"It's too hot for me. I'll take some lemonade. I already ate."

She served them and went away. Cammy thought to call after her. "Don't you want anything?"

There was silence. It filled Cammy with the memory of Patty Ann. For a minute, she almost couldn't eat.

Andrew saw her face and said, "Cam, you didn't say anything wrong. Stop being so sensitive all the time. Both of you."

"Well, she makes us like that!" Cammy whispered. She took hold of Gram's hand and, with her other hand, she spoon-fed Tut her soup.

"Oh, now there!" Gram said. "Effie always could make soup!"

They ate their soup and sandwiches. Cammy got Gram Tut some crackers.

"Want to know what hurts?" Gram asked them, once she'd had a few sips of vegetable soup.

"You hurting?" Cammy asked. "Where?"

"In my head," Gram said. "I can make this-a room just spin around."

"Mom says it's a little vertigo," Andrew told Cammy.

"What's that?" Elodie asked.

"It means off balance," Cammy said.

"It starts in the inner ear," Andrew added.

Gram raised her hands shakily and held her head still.

"Are you all right?" Cammy asked her. "Here, let's eat the soup. Are you hungry?"

"Yes, starving," Gram said.

"Did Aunt Effie feed you?" Cammy asked softly.

"No."

They were silent. Even Andrew. They didn't know what to believe.

"You didn't have no breakfast?" Elodie asked her.

"No." *Any*. Any breakfast, Tut thought.

Effie wouldn't let me have it until I saw that child. Never did see her, Tut thought. But I smiled where I saw Effie look! She gave me the juice and egg, then, but kept the oatmeal for herself. Just selfish. Always was.

She wanted to tell sweet Baby D. But where was she all the time? Seemed like Tut never saw her youngest child anymore. Her head hurt her so.

CHAPTER FOUR

Sunberry Road

❧

THEY HEADED BACK to the pool with Cammy on the Rollerblades and Elodie on the bicycle. Cammy loved the skates and could go just forever on them, her arms swinging free. She wore the helmet. It was okay. They kept to sidewalks. They were both so bike-cool and steady; this way, they would never fall.

Elodie said she didn't feel good. "Think An' Effie poisoned me."

"Oh, hush it, copycat!" But Cammy had to laugh; El sounded so funny. "Andrew hear you, he'll freak!"

"Well, he can't hear me, can he? But my knee still hurts."

"You want me to pedal, and you skate?" Cammy asked.

"Nuh-uh, I might fall again," Elodie said.

"Well, I'm going swimming," Cammy said. Her cheeks felt hot. The breeze they'd had before had died away.

Elodie didn't say anything. Which, Cammy knew, meant she hadn't made up her mind whether she would or wouldn't swim.

"They see the Band-Aids on your knee, and . . . I don't know what," Cammy said. "You should've worn the knee pads when you skated."

"Well, I didn't," Elodie answered. And, whining, "They won't let me in the pool!" Pouting, "The lifeguards. They're strict about cuts and blood in the water."

Eh-ew! Cammy thought, and felt bad for thinking it. But blood in the pool! Then she had an idea. "Okay, listen up. I don't need to swim to keep cool. A long bike ride will do it. We'll go to my dad's."

"Noooo! You are kidding me!" El said, wide-eyed.

"My dad won't mind," Cammy said. "He told Andrew we could come and go whenever we wanted. Only I've never stayed the way Andrew and Richie have. I haven't been there in a while."

"Seems I was there one time after Patty Ann, a long time ago. Don't remember much. Girl, you kidding me?" Elodie asked. "Not his office, but his house?"

"I'm not kidding you," Cammy answered. Her dad's thirty-year-old house was all deep-shaded and sprawling. Down Sunberry Road, it was on the edge of town in the near-country. The garage he ran, for fixing cars and trucks, was in another part of town on a highway.

"Well, okay!" Elodie said.

"Let's go!" Cammy yelled, and started out on her Blades. She skated smoothly, easily, quickly hitting her stride. Elodie pedaled at her side. It was a swell, long way. Trees on either side of the road. Fields, off behind the trees. All was quiet. Just the sleek sound of her skates, and the bike tires, spinning. Their deep breaths on the heavy air. They went a good way in silence. And rode the heat with the gnats.

Cammy thought about no school and being free to roam around if they wanted to. Not long, though, school would start. She and El would go to middle school, seventh grade. *Scary!* she thought.

They were silent when they got to the house. Forsythia bushes on either side of a stone pathway. Large honey locust trees, still and shadowy dark in the yard. *Old place, my own dad's house. He says it's alive; says a house can do that. Live forever . . . inside you.*

"Coo-el." The house made Cammy feel good and safe to see it. Deep brown with white trim, it reminded her of the lodges in the park at day camp. Hidden in the trees, it had two stories and many windows.

"It's coolish here," came from Elodie, at Cammy's back.

"Damp, too," Cammy said.

Cammy went over to a fat, green metal frog in amidst the wildflower of Queen Anne's lace. She felt around under the frog and brought out a key.

"I was wondering how we would get in!" Elodie exclaimed.

"There's always an extra key, right there. My dad told me about it," Cammy said.

Cammy unlocked the door. Inside, there was a slight musty smell. The windows seemed to be closed; still, all was coolish, like the yard with trees. Silent rooms. But it was a friendly place. *Because Dad's so nice*, Cammy thought.

"This house is big," Elodie said. "Shoot, I could live in this place."

"As if!" Cammy said. She gave El a look. "Nobody lives in my dad's house but my dad, and maybe Richie, when he wants to, and Andrew any time he wants to." *I can, too*, she thought, *if ever I want to*. She didn't say it.

"Your dad got a girlfriend?" El asked.

"Duh-uh!" Cammy said. "Girl? You, stew-pid?"

"Well, he could have, you know."

"No, he couldn't!" Cammy said. "Duh!"

Elodie knew to let it alone.

Cammy didn't like to think about her dad and — she wouldn't even think it. But it could happen. Even not thinking about it made her swallow hard. Stare at the floor a minute.

Then she saw a light shining from the kitchen.

Hey! Somebody here?

CHAPTER FIVE

The House on Sunberry Road

❧

THEY LOOKED AROUND, but no one was in the kitchen.

"My dad must've left the light on. All the other lights are off, though," Cammy said.

They went back through the living room. It had a leather couch and two armchairs. There were tan curtains to the floor. Soft, tan carpeting. Then they went upstairs.

Her dad's room was at the end of the hall. Cammy went in. "He's got four windows all in a row. They look straight out on the backyard trees." They couldn't see much, until Cammy looked hard at something. "There's a car."

"Where?"

"There, on the side."

They pushed their faces against the warm window to see. There was a gray "rec" car — not really a car or a truck, either. Andrew called them "four-by-fours." She wondered about it. All shiny and new-looking.

"Your dad's . . ."

"No!" Cammy said.

"Well, whose, then?"

"I don't *know*!" Cammy muttered. "But there better not be anybody bothering around outside! This is my dad's place!" They saw no one. "Probably somebody's brought it over, to be worked on at Dad's shop," Cammy said. "Bet Andrew comes and gets it."

They crossed the hall to the other side. "Just the bathroom here next to my dad's bedroom and little bath; and then, there's another little bathroom and one more room." Extra towels were on the towel racks.

"You know all about this place, huh?" El said.

"Well, of course," Cammy said. "I could live here, but I don't care to." She rarely came over to her dad's. He came to her house, mostly, when he wanted to see her. Cammy thought coming to see her was also her dad's way of getting to see her mom more often. She'd figured it out all by herself. She grinned to herself about it, but told no one. It was her great secret dream to have her mom and dad come together again.

She was almost done showing the house to El.

The last door was closed. She opened it, saying, "Here's a smaller guest room with . . ."

She was about to say, "two twin beds," when she shut up.

A girl was lying on the bed closest to the door. A window was open above her. A fan in the window made a soft swishing sound, moving warm air from outside.

The girl looked steadily at Cammy. She had a flat black box like a laptop computer open on her lap. That's what it was. Her fingers were moving on its keyboard.

"Kids in this town don't know how to knock." Said in a low, husky voice.

Startled, Cammy stared, as the words sank in.

The girl wore black shorts and a striped shirt. At once, she struck Cammy as not so much pretty as striking. Her back was propped up against pillows. Her black hair, in thin twists, spread out around her. Shorter twists hung over her forehead. She wore tinted glasses, which made her look . . . well, different and smart — older.

This, so fast, coming in Cammy's mind. She was embarrassed about not knocking.

"Cat got your tongue?" the girl said. She smiled. But it didn't look friendly. Made Cammy feel bad inside. Jealous, for no reason.

There was another girl on the other twin bed. She had been still, sleeping. The second girl sat up, yawned, and stared at Cammy and Elodie. By now, Elodie had squeezed in beside Cammy. They stood there in the doorway.

Cammy thought, *Don't be impolite.* "My . . . I'm . . . I'm Cammy." Stammering. "Are you . . . who? Are you . . . ?" *A relative,* she wanted to say. She could've kicked herself. The girls, both of them, had to be cousins!

The second girl jumped up and turned a light on at a desk against the wall. She looked ratty. She was a short, stocky kid, with big, bright eyes, the color of burnt orange. Cammy had never seen eyes like that. They looked wild. Her hair was brownish, all puffy around her face, flattened a little on one side where she'd slept on it. She wore bib overalls cut off at the knees and a T-shirt underneath.

"Show-time!" The ratty kid started making rap moves — shoulders, high and tight; knees, bending; and arms, body-close, sweeping from side to side.

"She's Fractal Madison," the kid said to Cammy, pointing her thumb at the first girl. "Be ace-high; and awesome! Don't tell nobody, Fractal. But that's not her real name — y'know wuh-dum sayin'?"

The kid kept moving around, dancing to music only she could hear. "She act like she got no people. But it's just how she act. Huh! She be living wif me and my family. Fractal is *rad*. She *very* way cool."

"I live with Cammy," Elodie piped up, delighted by the girl. "But I got a mom and brothers . . ."

The kid stared at El.

"Hi, you all!" Elodie piped up.

The two girls studied Elodie, but they didn't speak to her. El clamped her mouth shut, confused and hurt.

Who are they? Cammy was thinking. *Not nice.* Then she thought of something to say: *I know who you are, I just don't know who you* think *you are!* She'd heard that from a kid once. Speak it as cold and hard as she could. Show them she wasn't some dummy. But what came out was, "I don't know who . . . you are . . ."

"You don't know from *chad*," Fractal, the girl on the bed, said.

"*Chad*," the dancing kid said, as if reciting. "Specks of paper that drop out of a computer card when it's punched." Knees bent, shoulders high. "Her real name be Jahnina Madison, but nobody callin' her that." She went on, as though she hadn't heard a word Cammy or Elodie had said. Arms moving, body twisting. "He-e-re's Fractal! She outta New York. Queens. Bofe of us. She and me, homies. We-all call her Fractal. What it is? I'll tell you sometime."

The girl, Fractal, laughed harshly at the other one, and said, "You don't *know* what it is!" Her accent was strange to Cammy.

"I know, I just don't remember," the dancing kid answered. They both laughed, like they had a joke between them.

They think we're dumb, crossed Cammy's mind. "Who are you all?" she asked, her voice too high.

The kid was looking straight at her, but ignoring her at the same time.

"And don't dare touch what Fractal carry in her backpack. Her box-ooter, scooter; her computer-duter," she said. "Woo-hoo!" She moved both hands tight together in fists before her. She seemed to be stirring an invisible bowl of something. Shoulders under her ears, her neck stuck out like a chicken's. *"She's a brainiac, brainiac!"* the kid sang. "A chiphead! Fractal rules!" And woo-hooed happily for no reason that Cammy could understand.

The one on the bed had a slight smile on her face. She watched through her long eyelashes. Every now and then, she touched the keyboard. "An' don't touch what be in her right front vest pah-ket," the dancing kid went on. "'Cause there's where she keep her little mo-dim when she be traveling."

More dim? Is that what she means? Cammy wondered. *It's a light?*

"When it on," the girl continued, "know wuh-dum sayin'? She surf wif-it. She working wif-it on nay-o-l."

Wif it? Cammy got some of the words. She'd heard of surfing, vaguely knew it had to do with what was called the Net. She did not know what a nay-o-l was. *Oh, wif — with it!* Cammy got it. *She's putting me on!*

Kids in Cammy's town said it slangy, too; *wif* it, jive-talking slang when they were just "chillin'" *wif* one another. Or *wit* it. *With!* But this kid had a different way of sounding, and the other one did, too. Cammy watched the dancing kid, while watching the other girl out of the corner of her eye. *Watching me*, Cammy thought.

"But now, she outta New York wif me."

"What's your name?" Elodie piped up again. She was looking at the ratty one eagerly.

The girl stared at her. "Who you be!" she said, finally, sarcastically. "Dag!"

Made El feel bad, Cammy could tell.

"I'm El," she said.

"She's Eloise Odie, called Elodie," Cammy thought to say.

"I'm El!" El repeated, raising her voice at Cammy. "You think I don't know who I be?" she said, already trying to sound like the ratty kid.

Shocked, it was Cammy's turn to be hurt. Who did El think she was, talking like that, yelling at her, in front of them?

"And who you!" Eyeing Cammy, the ratty girl spoke bluntly, like she was mad at something all the time. She never stayed still. She had stopped dancing and began to stretch and bend.

"I told you, once," Cammy said. "I'm Cammy. Cammy Coleman, from here. And this is my dad's house."

The girl on the bed rolled over on her stomach, which turned her back to Cammy and El. Carefully, she laid out a cord, which was plugged into the wall somewhere below the bed and the other end, into the laptop computer. Cammy's dad had one. He had another, a big office one, at the shop.

Suddenly, the short, stocky one grinned at Cammy. "We're first cousins! Your daddy and my daddy be half brothers — wuh-dum sayin?"

"What I'm saying," the girl on the bed spoke out, "is, you guys are *half* first cousins."

"Shut your mouf', you hinckty ditz . . . 'fore I —" the stocky one began, and stopped herself abruptly.

"Watch your own self before I *mung* you, girl!" the one on the bed said, not even bothering to look up from her computer.

But now the ratty kid was acting more friendly. "I'm Georgia Coleman, named after my daddy, George Coleman. But everybody come calling me GiGi since I was way little. I don't remember being here, but my Mom says I was, once. We with my daddy and my mom. They off with your daddy."

"What happened to 'wif'?" Fractal Madison said. GiGi ignored her.

"That's your car outside?" Elodie asked.

"That's our *riiide,*" GiGi said. "And brand coo-el."

"Somebody left a light on in the kitchen. Don't

you turn out lights in New York?" Cammy said, getting back at Fractal's "don't you know how to knock?" No way to start out with strangers who were cousins. But they made her mad.

"GiGi," Fractal said.

"Oooh, my bad. I did that, I left the light on," GiGi said. "Guilty as charged." She headed out of the room, with Elodie right on her heels.

Let her go — El — what do I care? Cammy thought. If Cammy left, too, she would just be following the leader. If she stayed where she was, she might find herself ignored by Fractal Madison.

Cammy let the door close behind Elodie. Fractal turned over, holding the laptop. She got comfortable, with her hands back on the keyboard.

She didn't look at Cammy. But she wasn't telling her to leave, either, exactly. She seemed to be focused on what she was doing.

Cammy slid down to the floor right next to Fractal. With all the excitement, she felt like she had to sit somewhere. She was scared, but she sat there. After all, it was her dad's house, and by kinship, hers as well.

Something about the girl was odd, quiet yet bold, too.

"How old are you?" Cammy asked, all of a sudden. It just slipped out. She held her breath.

"That's not *even* relevant," Fractal said. She snickered.

Dumber. Relevant? Cammy could have gone through the floor.

"I'm going on fourteen," Fractal said. She never looked at Cammy, but at the screen above the keyboard.

"You're thirteen! I'm twelve," Cammy said.

"Well, fab! — What d'you kids say — du-uh! You're a math whiz!" Her fingers tapped on the keys. "I'll be in ninth grade, though, next year. That's because I got the brains. Yeahhhh!"

Cammy felt awful. Why didn't the girl like her? If she kept talking, the girl would think she was a dweeb, a piece of nothing.

"Look! Look at this! Look!" Fractal Madison exclaimed.

"Me?" Cammy asked, and knew she was acting like an idiot. She saw Fractal's expression. Eyes, alive and shining behind her round glasses. Cammy leaned near and looked.

The lid of the laptop was the color monitor screen. Fractal's screen brought to light a place Cammy couldn't have dreamed. It pulled at Cammy; it grew. Cammy couldn't describe what she was seeing. "What is it?" she asked, barely above a whisper.

"Wait, girl," Fractal Madison said. "I'll make a movie out of it." A box, like a window, came on the screen. Fractal clicked her pointer on the word

"Render," then on "Make Zoom Movie." The image began to move, growing bigger and then smaller.

Cammy let out her breath. "Wow!"

"Yeah!" Fractal said. "I just downloaded this software a week ago."

Cammy didn't dare say anything. She didn't know any words for all of this. She knew software. She didn't know download. But what she saw was a fantasy of color and dark: a fat-bellied, pear-shaped figure all in black. It had many little pear-shaped figures just like it along its edges. The little figures were like black buds or knobs, of different sizes but all alike.

Fractal placed her arrow pointer on one of the buds, and the colors just exploded into spirals. On the spirals were tiny black spots with sparkles.

Cammy watched, openmouthed, as swirls of the black figure, the sparkling buds, came and went, deeper and deeper, smaller, then bigger. "Does download mean the Internet?" she managed, and held her breath.

"You download *from* the Internet. You are computer ill, child. I get to use this stuff for two weeks, free! But after that, only part of it will work and I have to pay for it — twenty-nine ninety-five. I ain't going to do that!"

"What will you do after two weeks?" *What stuff? The download?*

"Don't know." Fractal paused. "I'll say I don't want to buy it. I'll wait a couple of days and download it again! My time will be up by the end of next week, though, if I don't buy the software."

"You can do that?" Cammy asked. "I mean, say you don't want it and down . . . download it again?"

"I'll figure it out. It's shareware, though. All kinds of people you don't even know share it. You're supposed to pay for it if you use it forever," Fractal explained. "Don't like taking it for longer than I'm supposed to. But I'm just a kid, with not much cash flow!"

"Yeah," Cammy said, sympathizing.

Fractal's fingers tapped. "Here's another one of the Set."

Cammy stared. She didn't dare ask what was a set. It was just amazing. "It's such a pretty picture! And when you make it move, wow!"

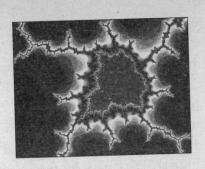

"You're looking at what's called the Mandelbrot Set," Fractal explained. "That pear-shaped black figure is called the Set because it has all these different parts to it, spirals, all kinds of things. I call it the black pear-man. It has some twelve different pictures to it in this software."

"Wow, it's sooo pretty!" Cammy said.

"Girl, it's called a mathematical marvel."

Cammy marveled at Fractal.

"They say it's the most complex object in math that makes this whole set of beautiful pictures. Maybe the most hardest thing anybody's ever seen. All these pretty pictures come out of one pixel. Know what a pixel is?"

Cammy shook her head.

"A pixel is the smallest little dot or mark of an image, of a graphic. Know what a graphic is I'm talking about? Like a picture on a computer," Fractal said. She didn't wait for an answer. "The computer picture has all these teeny-tiny marks that images are made of. And each mark is called a pixel."

"Uh-huh?" Cammy said.

"You get it?" Fractal asked.

"Yes! Sure!"

But Cammy wasn't sure she got it. It was beyond anything she knew. She turned her head from the screen to Fractal. What was on the screen seemed unreal to Cammy. And Fractal, too. *This kid,* Cammy thought. *Didn't know there was someone like her . . . Yesterday, didn't know — didn't, an hour ago. And now, I know. All that, inside a tiny pixel.*

There were a bunch of two-inch-square pictures with wonderful, awesome things in them when Fractal magnified them.

"Those things are Mande . . . what you said?"

Fractal laughed. "They are the Mandelbrot Set," she said. "They come out of this one black shape — the black pear-shaped man that Mandelbrot discovered inside a pixel. You can find them all over the Internet. They're on the sites of math people and scientists who make their own. This set was the second, done by a guy named Mandelbrot. Each picture in the set is called a — brace yourself — fractal!"

"Ahhh? You!" Cammy laughed happily. "You're a Fractal!"

"You got it. I'm Fractal, and the Mandelbrot Set

is fractals. That's about as much as I can tell. You can go, girl."

Cammy wasn't sure she'd heard right. The next second, she knew she had — when Fractal clicked something and closed the lid of the computer. She pulled out the plug.

Slowly, Cammy got up.

Fractal set the box on a cedar chest. Not looking at Cammy, she reached down, pulled the pillows up, and lay back down on her stomach. "You're the ones who drowned your cousin?" she said, muffled in the pillow.

Cammy couldn't believe her ears. She felt as if she'd come crashing down from someplace high. "We . . . I . . . never did!" Inside, her heart raced. Heat rose up her neck and filled her cheeks. About to cry, she groped for the door.

"Close it behind you, please, girl." Fractal lay still, at rest.

"I'm . . . Cammy! This is my dad's house!"

"Well, du-uh!" Fractal snickered. "But that ain't it! Heh, heh!"

It was the last thing Cammy heard as she fled from the room. She didn't care that the door slammed behind her.

She found Elodie outside. Sitting in the new four-by-four with GiGi. They were laughing and talking, all the windows down.

"El, I'm going!" Cammy managed. Her voice shook.

Elodie was in the driver's seat. GiGi had her bare feet out the passenger window. "I'll be there in a while," Elodie said.

"You've got my bike, remember?" Cammy said.

"I'll be there in a minute!" El said. "Me and GiGi are talking."

Cammy couldn't believe it. She stumbled out of there onto Sunberry Road. *All that wonderful sparkly stuff!* she thought. *Fractal gets mean in a minute! And Elodie — enemy! She can just move out of my house!* Tears dried on Cammy's face and neck as she skated hard and fast to home.

CHAPTER SIX

Home on Massy Street

⤮

HOME! *Glad to be here,* Cammy thought. She found her mom and Aunt Effie and Gram Tut outside in the narrow side yard. Away from the street, the grass was always greener on that side of the house. One big maple tree for shade.

The three women sat in the slant of coolness the maple made as the sun moved farther to the west. Gram Tut was in her wheelchair.

"Mom, hi! Nice, you brought Gram outside," Cammy said. She tried to sound okay. "Hey, Gram! I see you are making your beans! You make the best green beans!" Gram Tut was asleep. She aroused herself for a moment and gave a little smile. Then, she drifted off again.

"I might as well not be here," Aunt Effie said, not quite looking at Cammy. She snapped pole beans hard into the pan.

Cammy took in a breath, let it out; so did her mother, Maylene. *Aunt Effie's just spooky, and always will be,* Cammy thought. *But I did forget.* Before her mom could remind her of her manners, she said, "Hi, Aunt Effie." Cammy didn't dare wish her aunt away. She'd wished Patty Ann would do a *Star Trek* beam-me-up-Scotty, and look what had happened to her!

Stupid! Cammy told herself. *I didn't have a thing to do with that. No more bad thoughts. I've got enough trouble.*

"Air is just right for her drowsiness," Effie said, to no one in particular, but changing the subject back to her own mom, Gram Tut. Not often did Effie direct her words to Cammy.

Skating home had given Cammy time to calm down. Her face was still hot from the long way in the heat. But her tears were gone. Anybody seeing the streaks on her cheeks from her crying would believe it was sweat.

"Mom-mom-mom . . . ," Cammy said, and leaned over to hug her mom. Eyes closed, she breathed her mom's cologne scent, like roses, lighter than air. Opened her eyes. Her mom was so pretty — the same, every single day.

Maylene and Effie were about finished snapping

beans in a dishpan-sized metal pan. "You just get home?" she asked her mom.

"Been home a while. Cammy, your dad is coming to supper, with his brother and his brother's wife, and —"

"They are coming here, with . . . those girls?"

Her mom stared at Cammy. "It was a surprise. How'd you know GiGi . . ." She paused. "Oh. How did you happen to go over there . . . ?"

"Now Cammy's going to hide something," Effie said.

"Stay out, Effie," Cammy's mom said.

"Well." Cammy took a deep breath. "We went bike riding, El and me, only, it was boring." *Fib. Just a little lie,* she thought. *How was it Aunt Effie always knew she'd done wrong? But a small fib was better than the long tale about El's knee. They'd get in trouble.* "It was so hot, and I thought of Dad's house," Cammy explained. "He said I could come over anytime I wanted." That was the truth. "Showed me where the key was."

"You let her run wild like that, and her, *growing?* Anything might happen," Effie said. "Out in the country like that. Leave me in charge of her and Miz El Odie, and you won't have to worry."

Keep us penned up like two little pigs — with the big bad wolf, Cammy thought.

"Effie, please!" Cammy's mom said.

Effie clamped her mouth shut.

Gram Tut's mind clicked on. She was thinking back, seeing. Effie, please! I know this — the breakfast table, and Effie, going at it. So that I had to scold: Effie, please! Maylene asked for toast and butter. So Effie had to have two slices with *peanut* butter! Kicking at her little sister under the table. Effie, please! Saying she's the oldest, she gets more. But I begged, I scolded. I pleaded. Nothing made Effie be kind. Oh, it had to be my fault, somehow. Emmet: *Tut, don't blame yourself. She'll grow out of it.* Oh, Emmet! You know, she never did?

Her mom was waiting. "You went over there. And you met GiGi," her mom prompted.

"And the other one," Cammy said, now getting tearful.

"Oh, oh," Aunt Effie said. "I knew she'd find —"

"Take these beans inside, will you, Effie?" Maylene interrupted her. "They're about finished. I need to speak with Cammy."

"Well, what about Mom?" Effie asked, talking about Tut.

"Mom's sleeping," Maylene said.

"Takes two of us to get her inside, up those two steps." The side entrance had a door and a short hall to the dining room.

"I'll take care of it, Effie," Maylene said.

"After I do the beans, I got to get home for a while," Effie said, huffy all of a sudden.

"Well, be sure you and Earl come back about seven. You prepared well, Effie. Thanks for your help," Maylene said briskly, the way she could clear the air, like a cool breeze. "All I have to do is put it on the stove. You do so much. Kind of you."

That seemed to please Effie. Without another word, she took up the pan.

Cammy was on her knees by her mom's chair. Eyes closed tight, she buried her face against her mom. She held herself still until Aunt Effie went inside with the beans. Then she sniffled, crying softly. When she could stop, her mom asked what the tears were all about. And Cammy told as quickly as she could. "Asked me, did I drown my cousin. I said I never did!"

Maylene was quiet, still. Finally, she said, "Probably testing you out. Kids will do that in a new place. You be careful of her, Cammy."

"But she's no kid! They're all the way from New York-Queens. Think they're so tough!" Cammy said, sobbing. She had a vague idea what that place was like. She knew it was big.

"Okay, now stop, Cammy. You're all right. Everybody knows you didn't have anything to do with Patty Ann's . . . Listen. They have to be tough, GiGi and the other one. They go to big schools, all kinds of people, good and bad, in big neighborhoods, larger than this whole town."

"But who is she, that girl?" Cammy asked. She wiped her eyes. Felt afraid — what it must be like to live in a place like that.

Calls herself Fractal, but Cammy didn't say it. For some reason, she wanted to keep to herself the girl's fractals and the black pear-man figure. If Fractal told, it would be all right, but Cammy sure wouldn't tell. Suddenly, the thought dawned: Maybe Fractal had waited for GiGi and El to leave — on purpose so she could show Cammy the pear-man. Maybe being tough was Fractal's way of making friends.

She realized suddenly that her mom hadn't answered. "Mom? Is she a first cousin, like GiGi?"

Her mom sighed. "She's over there on George's mother's side. Mother was Tillie. George and your father had different mothers." Maylene was silent a long moment, then said, "She's George's mother's sister's . . . daughter's . . . daughter."

"Wow!" Cammy said. "All that? What is she to me?"

Her mom hung her head, smoothed out the dress she'd been wearing the whole day. Finally she said, "A relative . . . like everybody else is."

Cammy felt relieved. She guessed she wanted Fractal as a cousin. But not a close one. Not a first or second or even third cousin, but just a cousin.

Cammy then told about Elodie and how she'd

just stayed there in the car with GiGi. "I could see they didn't want me around," Cammy said. Her mouth puckered, turned down, like she might cry again.

"Cammy, Elodie has a right to be friends with someone else, too," Maylene said.

"I know it," said Cammy. "It's just . . . we've been around together every day this summer. And now, GiGi and . . . the other one." *They had to come and spoil everything!* she thought. And said, "The other one's Jahnina."

Her mom was quiet, too long.

Cammy leaned back to see her face. "What?" Cammy asked.

"Nothing. I was just getting everybody straight. She lives with your Uncle George and his family." Her mom, talking fast about Fractal. She gave Cammy no time to think about what she was saying. "Don't see them often, only at reunions. And George felt . . . it might be good for rambunctious GiGi to have somebody with her. There!"

Cammy stared at her mom. Maylene smiled suddenly, cleared her throat as though to clear the air. "GiGi's a whole dance team, all by herself!" She hugged Cammy. "But you'd think New York would be worse. Well, that's not my business!" Maylene smiled, yet her voice sounded tight inside her. "Too many stories," she finished, and kissed Cammy on her forehead.

"I want to know all the stories."

"Well," Maylene said, "you'll hear stories. Maybe not the way you think. You'll see."

It came to Cammy that maybe she'd missed something. Something in the way her mom talked that she didn't quite understand. She couldn't ask Maylene anything because she didn't know her own self what she didn't quite get. When she looked hard at her mom, she couldn't see anything different. She let it go, as a rushing sound came toward them from the front of the house.

Elodie, coming around the house, all in a hurry, riding the bike in. She stared anxiously at them as she hopped down. She let the bike drop, looking from Cammy to Maylene; and gauging with her eyes, back and forth, to see if she was in trouble. Cammy sat herself on the ground beside Maylene. She began taking her skates off. "Forgot I had them on," she said.

That was when Elodie said to Cammy, "They're coming! All uv-um!"

"Aunt 'Lene," she went on, to Maylene, talking fast, "Uncle Morris an'em are all coming to supper!"

Du-uh! Cammy didn't even look up at her.

Maylene smiled. "I invited them," she said. "I thought it'd be nice to . . . to have them over . . . after their long trip." Carefully, not looking at Cammy as she said that. "They arrived last night.

"Elodie," Maylene added in that brisk, not un-kind way she had.

"Ma-am?"

"Uncle Morris shouldn't see how casually you throw down the bike. Cammy lets you ride it, so you do your part. Stand it up, please."

"Oh, sorry!" Elodie said, and kicked the stand down. The bike stood.

My new bike, my dad gave me, you crumb, you traitor! Cammy thought, forgetting all about no bad thoughts. Cammy placed her skates neatly next to her bike. El wouldn't look directly at her now.

Just like Aunt Effie wouldn't, Cammy thought. *Well, I won't look at El, either. GiGi — see if I care!*

"Who's coming? Who's here?" Gram Tut spoke out, all at once. She was wide-awake.

"I'm here, Gram!" Cammy said.

"Me, too," Maylene said, "and Elodie."

"Oh, I know that, heaven's sake," Gram said, "but who's coming? Is it the Union, here?"

"Yes!" Cammy exclaimed. "Part of it, anyway. My dad and Uncle George Coleman and Aunt — I for-get."

"It's Bessie," Maylene said. "You were little, the last time she was here. But we've spoken about her, I'm sure. It's Bessie Coleman."

"Bessie Coleman." Cammy repeated it so she would remember.

"And GiGi," Elodie piped up. "She's the daughter and my cousin."

"*Our* cousin!" Cammy said, trying to sound brisk
and sure, like Maylene. Thinking, *Why in the world
did we ever let El come here? My bad! But I get tired
of thinking nice. My brain's so full of . . . of stuff!*

Maylene talked to them. "There's going to be
company in and out in the next few days. I'll need
your help, to pick up after yourselves wherever you
go in the house. If you throw pillows on the floor in
the living room, put them back the way you found
them when you leave the living room. If I need you
in the kitchen, you drop everything and come to the
kitchen."

"But can't we play —?" Cammy began.

"With GiGi an'em," Elodie said.

"Of course you can," Maylene said. She lowered
her eyes. "I expect the . . . girls . . . will be over
here, and you'll be over there." She sighed deeply.
Was oddly still again, a moment.

Something, not like my mom, Cammy thought.
Now why is that?

Right then, Maylene said, "Maybe I can get you
all to pick me some greens."

"Huh? Yeah?" Elodie said.

Dumb! No! Cammy thought, and knew El was
thinking the same. "Mom! They aren't going to
want to do country stuff," Cammy said.

"I bet they like to eat greens. Miss Perry plants

them all through the summer and eats them to frost," Maylene said. "She's got so many, she said for me to come get some when my people come." Maylene smiled. "I'll need a mess of greens by Friday."

"What kind?" Elodie asked.

"Mustard," both Maylene and Cammy said at the same time.

Cammy laughed.

"Oooh, I love mustard!" Elodie said.

"Strick-o-lean!" Gram Tut spoke. "Jowl bacon!" They all turned to her.

She was grinning. Everybody laughed. Cammy knew strick-o-lean meant fatback bacon that had just a line, a streak (strick!) or two of lean bacon meat running through the fat.

"Now, you don't need much," Gram Tut added. "But you have to have a nice square junk of strick-o-lean in the pot if ever the mustard is going to *taste*."

"I'll need a couple of baskets," Maylene told them.

"El, you get GiGi." Cammy said it quickly.

"And you get Fr —"

"Jahnina," Cammy interrupted, before El could say Fractal. "I'll get her."

"O-o-kay!" Elodie said. "It'll work!"

Maybe it would, Cammy thought. *But how do you get somebody like Fractal to pick mustard greens?* This was Thursday.

Maylene got to her feet. "I want you both to help me with Mom and the chair," she told them.

Cammy slung the skates over her shoulder and got up. Maylene pushed Tut's chair to the side steps. Cammy and Elodie took hold of the front. They lifted as Maylene pulled the chair by its handles backward up the steps.

The wheels rolled up. They watched so that Gram Tut would not fall forward from the bounce. Cammy saw how frail she was. Gram barely filled the chair. She could see Gram's bony knees through her housedress. Gram Tut's skin was yellowish, like her hair. Both her skin and her hair needed the out-doors. *Lots of sun and air,* Cammy thought, aching for her Gram, so frail.

There was an odor to Gram. Old age. Old people . . . smell. Then Cammy felt bad, wondering if that were true. *El, don't you dare say: Ooooh, some-body stinks!*

But El was doing her job. She carried most of the weight from the front of the chair, saving Maylene from having to strain herself. Cammy put a hand on Gram's arm. Tut smiled, reached up for her. With her bony, scratchy fingers, she grabbed Cammy's hand.

That way, they went in the house.

"Work to do!" Maylene told them. "You all better wash up and put on some nice jeans for dinner. And be good now. It's going to be a . . . a somewhat taxing evening." Her face looked kind of sad to Cammy. But then she smiled brightly, said, "I'll need your help!"

She's thinking about my dad, I bet, Cammy thought. *Bet she's glad he's coming to dinner.*

"Mom, you change your dress, too."

"What's wrong with my dress?" Maylene wanted to know.

"Well, you worked in it, and you're cooking in it. Probably all sweaty by now."

"Shew! Listen to her!"

"Put on that pretty beige pantsuit."

"Oh, my! All right, I will. I was thinking about it anyway."

Good, good, good! Cammy thought.

Maylene took Gram to her room, talking to her. Gram was babbling back, happy to have her baby all to herself.

Cammy and Elodie took to the stairs, with Cammy in the lead, as always.

CHAPTER SEVEN

Family Dinner

⊷

THINGS MOVED. They happened even when you'd think they wouldn't. Things changed, even when time passed so slowly, it felt like pain. Cammy and Elodie got cleaned up in no time.

"Our bad," Cammy said. "Now, we have to wait."

They lounged in Cammy's room. They'd done everything Cammy's mom had told them to do: Straighten their beds. Dump play clothes in the hamper. Wash out swimsuits, wring them out in a towel, then hang them on hangers in Cammy's room to dry.

They'd hung up their hand towels. Put on clean socks and jeans and shirts with boat necks. Wore their new shoes! Emptied the wastebasket. They looked each other up and down. They stood in front of the long mirror in the hallway. And they primped at the dresser mirror, side by side.

"That's too much lipstick, El," Cammy said. "Take it off."

"Well, GiGi wears it."

Cammy had a tube of Earth Rose. "Mom says you put it on, then wipe it off with a Kleenex. It'll leave your lips with a *suggestion*," Cammy said.

"Suggestion of what?" Elodie wanted to know, sounding tough.

Trying to be GiGi, Cammy thought. "Suggestion that your lips light up your face!" Cammy said. *Dummy!*

Elodie giggled. "My mouth's a flashlight."

Cammy had to laugh, too. "El, you are so . . . so . . ."

"I am not!"

"You don't know what I was going to say."

Their voices rose up the scale. "You don't know, yourself, either!" Elodie yelled.

They pressed, shoulder against shoulder, trying to shove one another out of the mirror. "Wait!" Cammy said. "I have to put my flashlight on!"

Laughing, giggling, they got along. GiGi hadn't come all the way between them. Cammy still resented that GiGi had taken Elodie away. That was the way she thought of it. But now, in Cammy's room, they were close cousins again.

They settled down, and Elodie climbed up to the

top bunk. "My bedroom," is what she called it up there. Cammy turned on the radio, low. She slid onto her lower bunk; she lay down on her back, thinking hard. Seventies music played. Funny music. *"Bye, Bye, Miss American Pie . . ."*

"Hey, change that station." She heard Elodie but paid no attention. Fractal was on her mind — how smart she must be! Then, Cammy was dozing, sleeping. Elodie must've dozed, too.

But at some point, El was leaning over her. Poked her. "Cammy! They're here!" El ran out of the room.

"Fell asleep," Cammy said. No one answered. She heard voices.

Next she heard feet on the stairs. She sat up. Before she could get to the mirror to make sure she looked all right, GiGi bounced into the room. She was moving sideways, doing a sidestep routine Cammy had seen only on television. GiGi's mouth was going a mile a minute: *". . . you ever wanna be me, you know, you know, you know, you gotta see me . . . dance. . . ."*

"See me dance," echoed Elodie. She brought up the rear, delighted to be peeking around Fractal Madison.

GiGi pranced around the room. "Hi," she said. *"Killer diller, star power, in the spotlight, any hour — of the daytime or night. You know, you know, you can't stand it up, you got to hand it up — to me! Generation's Big G and G.*

"Not a bad room," she said. "My room is bigger. But it's in the ci-tay. Houses next door to us." She'd stopped dancing. But she still moved, up on her toes, then on one toe, hands over her head, touching. "Here, you have *room* . . . space. Coolness."

"GiGi, will you cut it? Can't anybody think," Fractal said.

"Oh, you be still yourself, Ms. Witchy-ditzy."

"Cammy, I'm going to show them the rest of the upstairs," Elodie said. "Come on, you guys." She turned and marched out. Surprisingly, GiGi and Fractal followed her. Left Cammy standing, not quite all herself and awake, in the middle of the floor. Fractal turned sideways, pulled at her backpack, and lifted up the laptop, just far enough for Cammy to see it. Silently, she mouthed, "Later."

Cammy managed to hold her smile back. She didn't want to be too eager. She nodded at Fractal as she went out the door.

We're going to do the computer! But when?

Cammy went downstairs. Everything flowed, moved. The girls came rushing, giggling down. The men were standing in the living room — her dad and Uncle George Coleman, Richie, Richie's dad, and Andrew. Aunt Bessie Coleman was with Maylene in the dining room. Gram Tut was already seated at the table. That was the way it was this summer. Gram Tut sat at the table while everyone else got ready, talking, laughing. Everybody but Aunt

Effie. She liked to stay out of things when there was a crowd. "Must be in the kitchen," Cammy whispered to Elodie.

"Stirring poison in the food!" Elodie whispered back. They had to hold themselves tight inside to keep from laughing.

Cammy and Elodie met Aunt Bessie and Uncle George. Cammy held her dad's hand. He put his arm around her, telling his brother that Cammy had grown more than an inch this summer.

"You don't remember me, do you?" George Coleman said to her.

Cammy heard herself saying, "No, I don't, sorry!" and he and her father smiled at her.

"Well, you were a little girl, then," George Coleman said. "Can't hardly recognize you now."

Uncle George was a sandy man, just like her dad. Not as handsome, though. And his sandy hair had turned gray almost all over. He was balding. He did have light eyes, just like her dad's. Bessie Coleman came up to her. "You look like Morris," she said. She peered hard at Cammy.

Cammy couldn't help smiling. She felt shy. "I do?" she said, for want of something to say. She felt stupid. Cat had her tongue.

"She's got his smile," Maylene said. "And going to have his height."

Cammy's mom was right there. Oh, she looked pretty in that sleeveless, beige pantsuit! Cammy had to back up to see both her dad and mom at the same time. Her dad was looking at her mom. Into her eyes. Her mom seemed flushed in the face. Her cheeks glowed.

"She's got his eyes, too," Maylene said about Cammy to Aunt Bessie.

She saw her dad watch her mom. Then Cammy saw Fractal watching her dad, her mom, too.

Next, Maylene was moving around, and so was Bessie. Andrew helped, bringing ice cubes in a bowl to the table. Richie was there, helping Andrew fill the glasses. Maylene and Bessie poured cider; Richie put a pitcher of lemonade on the table. Wherever Maylene went, Cammy's dad turned slowly to see.

The girls moved politely around the adults, accepting compliments on how they'd grown, how they looked. At one point, Cammy's dad and his brother, George Coleman, got hold of GiGi, then Fractal, and gave them hugs.

Cammy's face filled with smiles. She couldn't stop it. Her dad was hers! She touched her cheek as a smile came over her, clear down to her chin, her ears. She leaned over, talked to Gram Tut a minute.

"Too much noise," Tut said. "Why's everyone moving so fast? Slow down, where's the fire?"

"Oh, Gram!" Cammy said, laughing, and hugging her. "Love you!" she whispered in Gram's ear.

Her mom beckoned to her and El — go to the kitchen. They did, and found that GiGi and Fractal were already there, with Richie and Andrew. Aunt Effie had both girls in hand. It was clear they'd been giving sympathy to her about Patty Ann. Aunt Effie didn't want to let them go.

"I'm real sorry," GiGi was saying. "I wish I'd known her." Older now. No dancing anywhere in her legs. Her feet were planted firmly on the floor.

Fractal gazed at crazy Aunt Effie. It was like she grabbed Effie's feverish eyes with her own unreadable ones. "We heard all about how good she was. Know you miss her much," Fractal said. Her voice was low, rough at the edges. Her arms were folded tightly across her chest.

How was it that GiGi and Fractal Madison knew exactly what to say? Cammy wondered. They treated Aunt Effie like — like she was important.

"And never gets any better," Aunt Effie was saying. "I cry every day."

She wasn't going to let them go. GiGi knew what to do. Kiss Aunt Effie's cheek; give her a soothing hug. Aunt Effie took her hand. After a moment, GiGi slid her hand away from Effie's. Fractal did the same. As she hugged Aunt Effie, her back was as straight as a board.

"Well, let's get started." Maylene came in with Aunt Bessie. She didn't look at anybody, nor did she smile at Cammy.

Funny, Cammy thought. *She's nervous with all so*

many people. But she's a good cook. My dad makes her nervous!

Things moved swiftly after that, before Aunt Effie had a chance to cry or stare off. Cammy had seen that enough times. Richie put his arm around his mom. Andrew held her hand a minute.

It was one of those meals they seldom had. Maybe on a Sunday, at Easter, or at Christmas. There, on platters and in serving bowls, were Cammy's favorite meals rolled into a grand one. GiGi and Fractal were politely impressed. With Cammy and Elodie, they brought the spread to the table. Richie and Andrew carried extra chairs from different parts of the house.

When everything was in place, they all sat down at the big oval table, which took up most of the shortened dining room. The door to Tut's room was closed.

"You did yourselves proud," Cammy's dad said. She sat next to him, with her mom's place on her other side. Andrew was on her dad's far side. And next, down the table, was Fractal, then Richie and Richie's dad, and Effie's place, and Uncle George, GiGi, and Elodie.

"I want some of my beans," Gram Tut said.

"I have to bless the food first, Mom," Aunt Effie said.

"Bless it, then."

Gram was tired of waiting, Cammy could tell.

Aunt Effie made a short blessing. GiGi and Fractal each had folded their hands in prayer under their chins.

"*Blessed be this food, this family . . .*" Next, they had their napkins on their laps. The bowls of vegetables, coleslaw, salad, and platters of meat were passed around. Two kinds of gravy.

"Summer and winter food — it's late August," Maylene said.

"I do that, too, this time of year," Aunt Bessie said.

"Bessie, are you baking your cakes for the weekend?" Effie asked.

Everybody knew she was. Bessie nodded. "Umhum. Morris has a level oven. I need level and steady heat for my cakes."

"I have a level oven, too," Aunt Effie said pointedly. "You could use my oven."

Bessie didn't say anything, only nodded that she had heard Effie.

"Bessie can still bake best of anybody," Uncle George said. "Wedding cakes, all kinds of cakes."

"Hear that?" Bessie said. "*Still?*"

They all laughed.

"Can't wait," Andrew said.

"Effie makes the best potato salad," Maylene thought to say. "I can make baked beans."

"It's enough to make a man cry," Uncle George said.

GiGi squealed, "Oh, Daddy!"

"Well, it's true," Cammy's dad said, "particularly the baked beans."

There was a short silence in which Maylene wouldn't look at him.

"Who baked the rolls?" Richie asked.

"I did!" Cammy piped up. Elodie poked her.

"She did not!" El told Richie.

"I know she didn't. She's just talking," Richie said. "How you doing?" he said to Cammy.

"Okay," she said. She grew shy, with everybody looking at her. Someday she'd cook the food; so would Andrew, maybe. They'd watched Gram Tut, her mom, and Aunt Effie. Sitting in the kitchen talking, and watching them cook.

She smiled at Richie; he and she never seemed to talk much. She liked him, though, but she hadn't always. Hadn't last year, when he wouldn't work, when he drank a lot, and him, a year younger than Andrew. But after his sister, Patty Ann, drowned, Richie had gone cold sober. He was still sober, and pleasant, and sometimes serious, like her Andrew.

Baked ham and baked chicken, the way Gram always made it. Butter rolls, salad with tomatoes and cucumbers. Baked corn, which was a winter dish. Gram's green beans. Red gravy with raisins, to put over the ham. Chicken gravy with mushrooms, for the chicken. The dishes paraded around the table. Coleslaw was the best ever.

Pass the butter, please. Pass the beans. I'll take another piece of the chicken. Who made this chicken so tender!

Everybody talked, taking turns, eating. Passed their plates for more.

"Taste your beans, Gram!" Cammy said.

Tut took a little. But her mind was off somewhere. She held food in her mouth. Forgot to chew it. She couldn't place things, and stared at Bessie a long time. She gave up trying to figure out who she was. She didn't want to ask. The men looked like farmers. Emmet would know.

They are all relatives, he told her. She nodded, I see that now. The Union is coming. *It's on its way.*

They got full. The grown-ups had coffee and pumpkin pie at the table. Exclaiming over the pie. "Lighter than air, Aunt Effie," Andrew said. She nearly beamed at him. Talking, catching up with who of the elders had died. Who had been born of the youngest families. They ate Aunt Effie's pie. It was delicious. Grown-ups kept talking.

Cammy wanted to hear, but she wanted to go off with Fractal. After the two of them finished eating, Fractal gave her a look. GiGi and Elodie had already left. They'd been whispering at the table. Those two had gone outside, probably to sit in GiGi's family car, making up things. Cammy felt a twinge of jealousy. It left her when Fractal said, "Let's go somewhere."

Andrew watched them. So did her dad, looking slightly alarmed. He gazed at Fractal, with something like a warning in his eyes. *'Cause she's older,* Cammy thought. *He wants to know what we're going to be doing. He still thinks I'm a kid — am I?* She didn't know how to act around somebody like Fractal. With Elodie, she only had to be herself.

"What do you want to do?" she asked politely. Her dad was still right there. "I'll be back, don't go!" she told him. *You are going to have to sit here with Mom!* was what she thought. Her heart leaped. Her mom was looking down at her plate, then away. Wouldn't look at her and Fractal Madison.

"I'm not going, sweetheart. I'll let you know when I do," her dad said.

And made her proud that Fractal and everybody had heard him.

Fractal turned on her heel, away from the table. She looked grim. But when she spoke to Cammy, it was in a cool, calm voice.

"Let's go where nobody can bother us," Fractal said. "Where there's an outlet. We might need it."

They were in Cammy's room, by the window and the desk she and Elodie shared, and two chairs. Gingerly, she and Fractal squeezed in side by side, with the computer on the table before them. Cammy forgot, then remembered where the outlet was. She felt so nervous, dumb sometimes. She said that, out loud. Maybe Fractal would feel sorry and have pity on her.

"You're not dumb," Fractal said. "You just haven't found out stuff."

"Yeah," Cammy agreed, and felt good all of a sudden.

"To get smart, you gotta learn," Fractal said, climbing the stairs.

Cammy looked at her. "I thought you had to be smart first before you could learn."

"It's what most kids think," Fractal told her. "But it's learning stuff that makes you smart. Once you know all kinds of stuff, you can feel better about yourself." She opened her computer. "So, what'dya think? Where shall we go? There's a lot to see out in the cyber world."

"To the mandi-brought set," Cammy said, getting it right, she thought.

"Well, good for you! See? You learned something with just one lesson," Fractal said. "We'll plug into the outlet, but we don't need a phone line, I don't guess."

When Cammy looked, questioning, Fractal said, "My Mandelbrot software runs like any program. We don't need a modem for it."

Cammy stayed quiet, not understanding or knowing what to ask. Then she thought of something to say. "Thanks for teaching me."

Fractal nodded. "I'll be a teacher some day," she said. "Or a scientist. Maybe I'll teach science. Kill two birds with one stone — know what that means?"

"Means you can be both — a scientist and a teacher rolled in one."

"You got it, girl," Fractal said.

Cammy looked at her. "My name is Cammy. Camilla. Don't call me girl, please."

"Cool, Cammy. See, I learned you like to be called by your name."

Feeling sure of herself, all at once, Cammy said, "I learned you like to give tests."

"Hey, there! You learn fast," Fractal said. Still, she didn't smile.

But Cammy did a smooth cartwheel in her head.

"This is called booting up," Fractal said. They watched the computer screen. "Programs are loading." Windows 95 came on the screen and filled it with color.

"That's a graphic, like I was telling you about," Fractal said.

The graphic disappeared, and little cartoony pictures appeared on the screen.

"Those are called icons, symbols for different programs," Fractal explained.

Cammy saw a green pyramid with AOL written under it. There were others. "What's —"

"Just look and listen for now," Fractal said. "I'll teach you a little at a time. You know what I found out last night? I found this page where the guy set up his own fractals. And a fractal art museum! He lets you put in your own numbers and then shows you the fractals it makes. It is so cool!

"But I couldn't make any fractals," she went on. "He's all full up. So many people want to put in their numbers. I have to wait. He puts the date up." She paused. "You can talk now," Fractal said.

But Cammy didn't know what to say. It was like getting a jolt in her brain, every time Fractal told her something. It was hard to keep everything straight, she was seeing and hearing so much that was new.

Wonder if Elodie is learning anything. Not like this, though, Cammy thought. She imagined GiGi and Elodie girl-talking, clothes, hair, boys. She liked to do that, sometimes, herself.

Swiftly, Fractal clicked a Start button. She clicked on an icon called "Software." Cammy didn't catch all the words. And there on the screen came the Mandelbrot Set. "Click on that one," Fractal said. "Put your hand on this round ball at the front of the keyboard. On bigger machines, it's on a cord, and it's called a mouse. Real new machines are even different still."

Cammy knew that. At school, the computer she

used for math games had a mouse. But she didn't say anything.

"See, the ball moves the arrow on the screen. It's called a cursor."

Cammy nodded. She knew all that.

"Then, you click the little bar in front of the ball. The deal is to point with the cursor and click with the bar."

Cammy did it all. She made a picture fill the screen and get smaller. She moved all over the black pear-shaped figure on the screen, making strings of sparkles grow into great swirls and eddies. It took her breath. She shook her head.

"See, here's a picture of the pear-man that's a model of the whole Mandelbrot Set," Fractal said.

Cammy clicked on the picture. Printed below it were the words: "Mandelbrot Set." *I didn't know how to spell it,* she thought.

"What I need," Fractal was saying, "is to get the software, else I won't get to study the Mandelbrot. My media specialist can buy it on a credit card, but I have to give her the money for it in front — know what that means?"

"Sure," Cammy said. "You give her what it costs *before* she does her credit card."

"Yeah, and she'll do that for some of us, like me," Fractal said. "For serious learning stuff. They have this program that lets us get all kinds of books and computer stuff. But I only have half the money. I've got until next weekend to get the rest. We go back this Sunday night . . ." Fractal's voice trailed off.

Cammy didn't take her eyes off the monitor. She didn't think much about money in the summertime. She got an allowance, which she saved up for presents, mostly. She didn't spend much otherwise; maybe a soft drink or some ice cream. A movie, now and then. She loved birthdays. Now, she heard herself saying to Fractal Madison, "I could lend you the other half."

"You could? I need about fifteen dollars."

Cammy thought that was a lot. She didn't say so.

"An'en, you know what? When I get back to New York, we can e-mail back and forth — get it? Electronic mail on the computer."

"But I don't have a computer."

"Yes, you do — right on Sunberry Road!"

"My father's? But he's not gonna let me —"

"How dya'know! Did you ever ask? No, huh? You're not into it? I'll talk to him. You talk to him, okay?"

"But when?"

"Kid, whenever. Tomorrow, soon. Friday."

Friday. Cammy thought about it. The Mandelbrot had her deep in the universe of it. Never before had she been so far away from home, and she hadn't moved out of her chair.

Friday. "You know what?" Cammy murmured. "Have you ever heard about picking mustard?"

"You mean, like, pick Grey Poupon mustard?" Fractal looked confused.

Cammy grinned; giggled. She'd seen the Grey Poupon commercials. The fractal before her on the screen bulged and thinned again. Fractal Madison sat with her, letting Cammy make all of the computer's moves.

"No!" Cammy said. "Not like that. Not like Grey Poupon," she said. "I'll have to teach you, too!"

"Oh, yeah?" Fractal said.

Cammy learned that Fractal hardly ever smiled. But that didn't mean she wasn't having fun.

"Hey!" Cammy shouted.

"What! You can get loud! Chill, Cammy!"

Calling me Cammy again! "You know what?" Cammy asked.

"Well, what!" Fractal got just as loud.

"See?" Cammy cupped her hands around the ball in its little mousepad, which drove the arrow cursor on the screen. "When I work it, it's a country mouse!"

"Oh, muh — you mean —" Fractal whooped. "And a city mouse when I move it! Oh-muh-gawww . . . !" For a moment, they seemed exactly the same age. They stared at one another, the black Mandelbrot wrapped in diamonds on the screen before them. They shrieked hysterically. Cammy had tears in her eyes. It wasn't anything. But country mouse, city mouse! Mice, twice! She and Fractal Madison. It was way rad!

CHAPTER EIGHT

At Miss Perry's

✤

SMALL INCIDENTS grew and changed in Cammy's head. She felt excited, nervous. It was awful, she was thinking, when you had to be at your best. When you had to hold still and seem like you were thirteen. You pretended coo-el when you were still twelve and knew nothing.

When Fractal and GiGi started fussing again, Cammy had to be calm and collected. Acting as if she knew how to be when she never did. Neither she nor Elodie ever were quite sure how they should act around the cousins from New York-Queens. They wouldn't look at one another.

All four of them, Cammy Camilla Coleman, El Elodie Odie, GiGi Georgia Coleman, and Fractal Jahnina Madison, were sitting at the kitchen table in Miss Alice Perry's house. *Would you believe it?*

Cammy thought. *Four of us, two city mice and two country, out picking greens! Mustard patch full of mouses — eeek!*

Politely, so as not to start anything, Cammy had told the two city-ditties how to hold their knives. There, among the mustard plants, she showed them how to bend or squat, how to turn, swivel with their feet. She showed them how to get under the mustard at the point where the stems came out of the ground. Cut the stems there. Showing how you sliced them without cutting yourself. And then, how to lift a mustard green on the knife and toss it into the basket.

"So that's where 'you can't cut the mustard anymore' comes from," Fractal said. "Meaning, you've gotten too old to bend and squat!"

"Dag . . ." GiGi said.

"Yeah, gad!" Elodie said. "I mean . . ." Confused, she giggled miserably.

Stew-ped! Cammy thought, about Elodie.

The ground was hard-packed and light brown. No rain. Mustard greens were dusty. They had been watered maybe yesterday by Miss Perry. The ground was damp right under them. The greens pricked you when their slightly fuzzy leaves touched your fingers. Greens glowed in the sun. Knives sparkled. Elodie's eyes were so bright. There next to GiGi, El couldn't think of a better place to be. Cammy could tell, and felt sad about it. El, even afraid to move for fear it wouldn't be a GiGi move, and she'd get it wrong.

Whatever, Cammy thought. She held her feelings in tight. After a moment, she explained, "When the baskets are full, we put them under the hose and wash the greens right in the baskets. We toss them like a salad to make sure we get all the dust and dirt off. Then, we set the baskets in the shade until we're ready to leave. Miss Perry will want to visit with us."

The gnats annoyed them, darting in and out of their sweat. GiGi was irritating, complaining — "Shoot, this is slave labor. Gad, my mama see me with a knife in my hand, doing this —"

"Hush up," Fractal told her. "You ought to be glad you can smell the ground and the fresh air."

"Well, I ain't glad," GiGi said. "It hurts my knees, like this. I can feel my sinuses going crazy."

"First time we've taken a deep breath in two years," Fractal said.

Cammy laughed, thought she must be joking. But Fractal never smiled. She was deep into the mustard, right next to Cammy.

"I'm telling you, this is cutting up my knees, and I'm a dancer!" GiGi said.

"About as much a dancer as I am a bird that flies," Fractal said, not mean but certain. And said it softly, as if she were telling only herself and Cammy.

"It'll be all right," Cammy said, just as softly back. She knew everything that was happening, but she felt as if she were outside herself, watching. Letting minutes flow and change in and out of her head. She had the fifteen dollars that Fractal needed on her mind. How was she going to get that much money? She had about nine dollars. And anyway, she had been hurt by something Fractal had done that morning.

Andrew had dropped Fractal and GiGi off at Cammy's house around 9:30. Cammy still had sleep in her eyes. She and El had stayed up late watching reruns. But the moment Fractal and GiGi had gotten out of the truck, they'd been fussing. Andrew had mouthed, "They're all yours!" He'd grinned gleefully at Cammy as he'd driven off.

"Leave me alone, girl!" GiGi had shouted at Fractal.

"Well, act right, then," Fractal had told her, shoving GiGi forward.

"Quit it! I ain't picking no greens!" GiGi had kicked at her.

"Yes, you are picking some greens — don't you want to learn something? You've never done it before, so you'll learn some'um-some'um."

GiGi had kept saying she wasn't picking greens. And the next thing Cammy knew, the two girls from New York-Queens had begun kick-boxing, for real. It had been serious, hard, foot-in-shoe hitting on the ankles and shins. Cammy'd never seen girls do anything like that. It had scared her. Then, Fractal had gotten GiGi in a hammerlock, and GiGi had pulled Fractal's hair and had bitten her hand.

"Owww!"

Cammy could still hear Fractal's shocked hollering in her mind. And Cammy had told them to stop fighting or she was going to tell Maylene.

It was then, Elodie'd had to get into it, saying something — "Oh, you're always telling on somebody. Your mom's gone to work already."

Cammy had told Elodie to just be quiet. "Go home!" *Awful thing to say. I didn't mean it! Sorry!*

For, suddenly, she'd seen a forlorn, scared look come over El.

Just as fast, things had changed again. GiGi, looking at Cammy, saying, "Oooh, dag!"

Fractal telling Cammy, "Bad on you, girl!" Smirking at her. All at once, saying, "Come on, Elodie, let's get her!"

"Yeah," GiGi had said, "get her!"

Elodie's face had lit up. It had happened so fast! They were going to get Cammy. She'd started running even before she knew it. Then she was inside the door, hearing them laughing at her.

"She can move when she wants to," Fractal had commented.

I hated them! Cammy thought now, sitting at Miss Perry's table. Angry, jealous, her heart had been in her mouth.

Then, the three of them outside — Fractal, GiGi,

and Elodie — had begun flinging one another, playing statue, and grabbing and pulling. Until they were all three on the ground, laughing and ducking their heads, and giggling. And lying still, even Fractal, looking long-legged, skinny, and older. Finally, they'd rested, cousins, with the sun and shade on them.

Cammy had watched through the window. What had happened? How was it that they had suddenly picked on her like that? And Fractal acting as bad as El and GiGi. *But then, I was wrong,* Cammy thought now. *I hurt Elodie.*

Cammy had made her way over to Miss Perry's. She hadn't cared if they came along or not. She had taken the two empty baskets with her. Maylene had put paring knives for each of them inside.

Cammy had felt the way she did when Patty Ann was alive. Like she was the one who wasn't as good, or smart. *Why'd they turn on me like that, though? I thought Fractal and I were getting along. Are they all my enemies?*

It wasn't long before they had come over, with Fractal leading the way. They'd spoken to Miss Perry a moment. She'd told GiGi she should have worn long pants.

"See, I told you," Fractal had said. Cammy could still hear that familiar smirking way Fractal had of speaking sometimes.

"Oh, shut up for five minutes!" GiGi had said.

Fractal, laughing — "Heh, heh!" it sounded like.

When the three of them had come in the field, Cammy was already at work. They'd stood around quietly. Elodie wasn't about to move until GiGi moved, until Fractal had said, "Tell us what to do." Fractal'd had her hard voice back. Polite, though.

Cammy had told them. Gave out the paring knives. Everybody had started working. It had been more fun than labor, Cammy thought now. She and Elodie were good at it. Fractal had gotten the hang of it. GiGi would've rather been anyplace but here.

Talking casually, all of them. GiGi, fussing about nothing. Fractal, telling her some'um-some'um. Nobody on anybody's case or side, and the "get Cammy" all but forgotten. As the morning had worn on, there on the dusty ground and in the weeds, in the greens, Cammy had calmed inside. The four of them, not yet close, a little wary. But once more, altogether cousins.

The day, turning. Them, sweating in the midst of heat and gnats, getting tired. Elodie had said, "It must be noon. We worked two whole hours!" And they had.

Now, their work finished, they sat in Miss Perry's old kitchen. It looked as if it were from another time. Wallpaper of little pink flowers. A brown table with a lace cloth. A clear plastic cloth over the lace. An electric stove. An old refrigerator, the narrowest Cammy had ever seen.

"Got something fer ya," Miss Perry said as they came in. She'd called them to come in when she saw them hosing the greens with her garden hose. Called sweetly in her voice that was usually raspy, "Cam. Cam. You bring your cousins. I got something."

Cammy liked the way Miss Perry spoke. She sounded old-timey. You felt she'd taken you to some long-ago, pleasant place when she talked only to you. They'd gone inside to the kitchen and sat.

"Going to like this," Miss Perry told them as she filled bowls from a big pot on the stove. There were her greens she'd cooked. She'd added hard-boiled eggs to them. The eggs were sliced in thin circles, like little suns. And she had seasoned the "pot likker" with wine vinegar.

Oh, man! At once, Cammy and Elodie got up and brought the warm bowls to the table.

"Oooh! I didn't know we would eat!" GiGi said.

"Dinnertime!" Miss Perry said. "You all call it lunch, I think. A little bit of what you'll be getting on the weekend. I don't have family to cook for now. Suppertime, I eat alone — I don't mind," she said. "But there's something about dinner I don't like by myself too much." She laughed. "I like to make special for Cam, while her mama, Maylene, be working."

Cammy grinned. She'd always been special to Miss Perry. She had to remember to come visit her. She'd forgotten for a long time.

"Thank you!" Fractal said. "Ummm! It has the best smell!"

Miss Perry opened her oven and brought out steaming corn bread. She turned the corn bread pan over on a serving plate. She clunked the pan bottom with a heavy spoon, and the bread came out on the plate in one piece.

"Gad! Ooooh, that's so way cool. Ummmm-huuum!" GiGi exclaimed.

"Cam, you cut the bread," Miss Perry said, handing her a knife. Cammy cut carefully in equal pieces. She put the pieces on their napkins.

"There's whole kernels of corn in the corn bread!" Fractal said.

"Always is," Cammy said, "and green onion. The little red pieces are sweet red peppers cut up real fine. My mom makes it just the same way."

"Taught her how," Miss Perry said.

They had a hard time eating for groaning with the wonderful taste of the food. Miss Perry brought them cider in blue paper cups. It was like a birthday party. They sat up straight, like children. They were polite, passing the corn bread and butter. They all felt the same, pampered and cared for. Chewing and swallowing, loving the greens and hard eggs, they giggled about nothing, almost choked. Miss Perry touched their hair, picked pieces of weeds out of it.

"Did you wash your hands? I didn't see anybody wash their hands!" she told them, smiling.

"Oooh," GiGi said, gracefully shaking out her hands.

"Gad, I forgot," Elodie said.

Making noise, giggles, they pushed their chairs back and rushed to the sink. "Look at my hands!" Cammy said. Nails, caked with dirt. Four pairs of dirty hands outstretched under the faucet. Cammy turned on the water, made it comfortable. She took up the soap, used it, and passed it from hand to hand. They watched their dirty, soapy water go down the drain.

Miss Perry gave them a dish towel to dry their hands on. They hurried back to the food. The corn bread was still warm. Fractal ate three pieces.

"Am I eating too much?" she asked Miss Perry.

Miss Perry sat with them; laughed at Fractal. "Never too much. Take it until you've had enough. Say, when you're full, 'I have dined sufficiently!'" It seemed to please her so, that they were there in her kitchen and that they liked being there.

When they had finished, and the table had been cleared off, Fractal reached into the backpack at her feet and took out her computer. They all were still at the table. "Can we go?" Elodie asked impatiently. Cammy knew she meant Elodie and GiGi — *Can we go! Well, let her, who cares!*

"Wait," Fractal said. "I want to show Miss Perry something."

"You can show her," GiGi said. "You don't need

us. Miss Perry!" GiGi exclaimed. "Thanks for a wonderful lunch!"

"Wasn't nothin' to it," Miss Perry said. "You come on over any time you feel like it. You and Elodie."

When they'd left, Miss Perry said to Fractal, "What you have to show me?" She seemed surprised one of them would want to show her something.

Fractal explained, and asked Miss Perry if she might plug her cord into the wall outlet. Miss Perry said she could.

The machine booted up. The screen made a high, tinny sound. It filled with color.

"Oooh! A little television!" Miss Perry said.

"Like one, sorta," Fractal told her. "This is a computer you can carry around with you. A laptop. I can use the battery, but I think it's run down."

She mentioned the modem, that it was for getting on the Internet, but that was all. Miss Perry said, "Um-hum, that's something. I heard a-that."

"We don't need a modem to use the software program," Fractal reminded Cammy. "Use a modem, you have to have a phone line."

Cammy nodded. She stayed quiet, listening and learning.

On the computer screen, there came the Mandelbrot Set. The black, round pear-man figure with buds, knobs, and distant, sparkling diamond strings, edges. Fractal zeroed in on a section of a glistening yellow edge at a boundary of dark. Cammy and Miss Perry fell into the universe of tiny locations. They fell even farther as nearly invisible details magnified before their eyes.

"Oooh, what kind a-place is that?" Miss Perry said. "Making me dizzy!" She scooted her chair away. "Like a black cloud, oooh, I'm fallin' in the lightning! The things television will do to ya," she said.

"It's . . . it's . . ." Fractal began. She brought up a wild pinwheel of colors; then rendered it in motion, a zoom movie.

Miss Perry watched. Her face relaxed. She grinned. "That's awful pretty! Reminds me of the northern lights!"

"It's a real small thing," Fractal said. "You couldn't see it with your eye. You have to have a computer to make it big enough to see." She changed the picture to another image. Suspended there in the blue was a tiny, black pear-shaped figure, upside down. "I just wanted you to see it," Fractal told her.

"Well," Miss Perry said. And got up. "A computer! With that little television screen? Huh!" She smiled. "I remember once when the northern lights filled the whole sky, and I have not ever seen that on television. They say there's nothing that television can't do. No, indeed! I go to church every Sunday!"

"We have to go," Cammy said quietly. She felt sorry, she wasn't sure for whom — for Fractal or

Miss Perry. Somehow, the Mandelbrot Set had no place in Miss Perry's kitchen. The out-of-time of iron pots and skillets, of yellowing wallpaper and fading curtains, was far gone from jeweled edges. And from the pear-man, repeating his dark shape endlessly in the fractals set.

They left. Went to where they'd put the baskets in the shade. But the baskets were gone. *GiGi and Elodie must've taken them,* Cammy thought. They would give the baskets to Aunt Effie to take care of. A way to get by Aunt Effie and into Cammy's room to talk and laugh secrets, was what Cammy figured. She didn't care. She and Fractal started out, cutting across Miss Perry's property. "She liked your computer," Cammy thought to say.

Fractal shook her head. "Don't think so. She didn't get it," Fractal said. "It made me mad. I couldn't make her see —"

"But she did see," Cammy said.

Fractal shrugged. "Someday, I'll be a teacher, and I'll know how to teach seniors," she said. "Seniors are hard, some ways. They don't want things shaken up."

"Teaching isn't easy, sometimes," Cammy said.

"You don't know from *chad or chomp*!" Fractal said, a hard edge to her voice. She'd turned on Cammy that fast.

Cammy's hurt came just as swiftly. She felt punished, as if she'd been thrown out of class. Standing in the hall for everybody to see.

So mean! I hate you! She didn't say it. Afraid of what Fractal might do if she said it. But she found herself asking, "What is 'chomp'?" barely above a whisper. She scrunched her shoulder, warding off an invisible blow.

To Cammy's surprise, Fractal answered. "It means, you lose," she said. "You've chewed on some'um-some'um of which you bit off more than you could *chomp*! Heh-heh."

Cammy didn't get it right away. But then she did. "Oh!" she said.

"See," Fractal told her, "computer lingo is short and sweet. It's KISS and tell. KISS — means, 'Keep It Simple, Stupid'!"

She guessed Fractal was calling her stupid. At the same time, Fractal was teaching her stuff she'd never heard of before. They continued on together. Cammy felt bad, dumb, and kept her eyes on her moving feet.

"Hey," Fractal said. Her normal voice was back, and soft, yet rough somehow.

Cammy looked up, trying to act as if nothing had happened. That was the way Fractal acted. Her glasses glinted at Cammy.

"I say we go over to my place. I mean, your dad's. Get his computer, and I'll show you a few things. We put you on the Internet."

"He won't want me to take his computer," Cammy said.

Fractal looked down at her like she was some kind of little puppy you petted. And she did pat Cammy on her head. Made Cammy laugh, to see how fast Fractal could be nice to her again.

"We're not going to *take* it! Yiddle booby," Fractal said. "See how foolish? You don't know what he *won't*, until you ask!"

"He's at work," Cammy said. She was afraid she'd get in trouble.

"I know where he is; we'll call him," Fractal said. "We just pick up the phone and give him a call. Easy as WYSIWYG — all caps." She spelled it.

"What in the world is that?" Cammy asked.

"Sounds like — wizzy-wig!" Fractal told her. "Means, 'What You See Is What You Get.' You don't see nothing, you know nothing."

"I never bother my dad. I never usually call him up," Cammy said.

"Man, yiddle mouse! Why you so scared?"

Cammy shrugged, still with a smile on her face. Fractal was half playing, half cajoling her, calling her a mouse. "I'm not scared, exactly," Cammy said. All she wanted was for her dad to keep on loving her. "I don't usually ask him for stuff. He gives me stuff when he wants to."

"Yeah? He does, huh?" Fractal was silent a long moment before she said, "Well, maybe he'd like you to ask once in a while."

Eagerly, Cammy looked blindly into the glasses at

the girl who seemed to know everything. But it worried her thăt she couldn't tell when Fractal would turn on her and hurt her feelings.

Fractal had both hands holding the strap of her backpack hanging from her shoulder. She calmly focused on Cammy. They were on the sidewalk now, and they stood there a moment. Fractal had her feet wide apart, her back straight. She could have been some dark, tall figure in a foreign land. Content in a desert somewhere. Long, slender legs. Behind the glasses, eyes like Cammy'd seen in pictures of ancient Egyptian girls.

Everything she does, Cammy thought, *all she is. Why can't I be like that?*

CHAPTER NINE

Relatives on Sunberry Road

❧

FIRST, THEY WENT home to get Cammy's bike. Without telling anybody, without seeing anyone, they took the bike from the side yard and started out.

Fractal pedaled, and Cammy sat on the seat, holding on to Fractal's shirt. They'd fastened the backpack on the front handlebars. But Fractal wasn't experienced on a dirt bike, or any other kind, Cammy decided. At the end of the street where they had to turn, she nearly wrecked them. The bike wobbled; Fractal had to jump down fast. She didn't say, "Oh, sorry!" She just got off the bike and grabbed her backpack. Stood there.

Looking straight through her little glasses at Cammy. No expression, hardly. She put her arms through the backpack straps and heaved it up her shoulders behind her. "What kinda bike is it, anyway?" she asked, sounding superior. She acted as if her own unsteadiness had been the bike's fault.

Cammy took hold of the handlebars. "It's got twenty-one gears," she said. "The grip shifters let you shift with just a twist of your wrists. It's got heavy-duty knobby tires. It's got a foam rubber saddle — that's the seat; and a Cro-Moly frame."

"Whatever," Fractal said. "I didn't wanna know all that."

Cammy's hurt was instant. All at once, she felt queasy. She swallowed; looked away. She wasn't sure, but she thought she could ride them both, standing up on the pedals. She might have to stop and rest. She'd see. Why hadn't she just stayed home?

"Okay, let's go," Cammy said, sounding tough. "Get on the seat."

"You got it, Mouse." Fractal carefully got on.

"Cammy," Cammy said.

"Cammy-Mouse," Fractal said. "Heh-heh." Her voice way down in her throat.

"Fractal City-Dittie Mouse," Cammy said, surprised at herself. "Keep your pant legs away from the wheel spokes."

They went. "Sit very straight!" Cammy said, over her shoulder.

"Kid, you just don't spill me," Fractal said.

But Cammy was good at this. She and Elodie, all summer long. They had toned their muscles to a fine tuning of strength. Coasting, she had the pedals at equal height. Her weight was even on each pedal. Her feet were steady on each. Seconds upon seconds, she glided them. She could feel Fractal's hands clutching her shirt. Next, she pedaled hard; then coasted again. Sweat, down her neck and armpits. Fractal's weight on the seat dragged at her muscles and pulled at her strength.

She struggled on down the hot, country road. An ache began, right in the center of her shoulders. But then —? What —? Something. She smelled the air. Coming. "Can you smell it?" she asked, over her shoulder. "The rain . . ."

"*. . . sliding down my wi-in-do-o-o-w,*" Fractal sang, in a surprising, melancholy tune.

Cammy recognized the melody. *Nice old song,* Cammy thought; then, *It's coming!* She looked up at the sky. She'd had eyes only on the road. A mass of black clouds! The wind came, rushing in front of the clouds. Rain would come down hard. Cammy let her muscles go and pedaled as fast as she could.

She saw the rain, streaks of it falling from dark clouds. Off beyond the fences and fields, it was falling in sheets, and spreading out over the land. A million mice scurrying through cornstalks was the sound of it. "Look!" she yelled. "It's coming! Wizzy-wig!"

Fractal tightened her grip. Cammy hollered, "Duck!" And, chin in, ducked her head down. She turned her face to the side, so the rain, when it hit, wouldn't blind her. She felt Fractal scrunch down.

The rain came, carrying a mist, like smoke. It hit them. Ran into them and flowed off them. It spilled over and through everything in its path. They were wet in seconds.

"Are we there yet?" Fractal yelled.

"In a minute!" Cammy hollered back. Now she was shivering. It was a cool rain. It made steam on the hot roadway. August, dog weather that could come and go in minutes. "Oh, man!" Her legs were tired now. But she was almost there. She wobbled the bike.

"Girl!" Fractal called.

Cammy didn't have time to say anything. It took all of her strength to hold the bike straight and not skid. She braked slowly, carefully, panting hard. They turned in between the soaked forsythia bushes of the yard. All at once, there was a gripping flash of lightning all around, and a giant, splitting boom over their heads. Cammy yelped.

"Ohhhhhh!" Fractal cried.

Cammy was off the bike. Fractal slid off the saddle. The bike crashed to the ground. They both ran, getting the door open. They were in. Her dad's house. Fractal, first. "Oh! Oh! I'm all wet!" Moaning, running her hand over her dripping hair.

"Yeah, it's got me all wet, too!" Cammy said.

They stood on the mat just inside the door. Cammy, wondering if they should drip themselves into the kitchen to get dish towels or get the stairs wet, running to the bathroom.

Fractal stiffened; Cammy sucked in her breath.

A girl Cammy had never seen was coming down the stairs. She carried neatly folded towels. "Shhhh!" she said softly, warning them. "Junie, my brother, is asleep — naptime. He's two. I saw you out the upstairs window," she went on. "You almost made it!" she laughed sweetly. "You got yourselves wet!" She had a soft, southern drawl.

"No kidding!" Fractal said, sounding cool and self-assured.

The girl hurried to Cammy first with the towels. "I bet you're Cammy," she said. "My mama said you had Uncle Morris's eyes. You do, too, huh!"

"I know you're a cousin," Cammy began.

The girl was wide and rawboned, looked country and older. "I'm Uncle Earl's side. He and my daddy are second cousins. My daddy is Horace Brecken-ridge. Everybody calls him Reverend Breckenridge, 'cause he is."

"Oh," Cammy said. "Uncle Earl is Aunt Effie's husband, and Richie's dad." In case Fractal didn't remember.

"Was Patty Ann's, too," the girl said. Suddenly

she covered her mouth with the towels in her arms. "Ooh, sorry," she said. Wouldn't look at Cammy.

What's she mean? Cammy wondered.

"What's your name?" Fractal asked.

"I'm Alise Anne Breckenridge. Don't you like that name?" she asked.

"Dim bulb," Fractal said under her breath. Cammy heard her. Fractal grabbed a towel out of Alise's arms and walked around her to the kitchen.

Cammy took a towel and said thanks. She followed the leader. The girl came on after them.

Fractal took her backpack off. Carefully, she lifted up her computer. "It didn't hardly get wet," she murmured. She wiped off the case. "Where you from?"

"Who, me?"

Fractal gave Alise a hard look over her bitty glasses.

"Knoxville, Tennessee. Got here this morning. My mama and daddy and Junie and me."

"How old are you?" Cammy asked. She always had to ask that.

The girl was silent a moment. "I'm big for my age," she said.

Something told Cammy not to ask anything more. Beyond telling her name, Fractal stayed quiet, too. She opened her computer and wiped it with the towel, making sure no wet got inside.

"Where did you get that thing?" Alise said. "How much did it cost? A lot, I betcha."

Fractal wiped her hair, face, and arms with the towel. "It's not a *thing*, it's a laptop computer," she said finally. "Kids get games and CD players, TVs. I wanted me a laptop."

"Huh!" the girl said. "Bet it cost your daddy, too!"

Fractal stared at the girl through her glasses. The three of them grew so still, they could hear the rain against the windows.

Cammy knew Alise couldn't see Fractal's eyes. She was learning, it was a trick Fractal played. Keep her face smooth and no expression. Look through her tinted glasses a certain way so you couldn't see her eyes hardly at all. It scared you. It kept you unsure about her.

There was thunder, rumbling off, as the storm passed beyond them, and the rain slacked. A new rumble hit the back steps. The back door flew open, and a big man clomped in. Wet, short-sleeved shirt, wearing a black tie. He wiped his feet on the mat, holding on to two big grocery bags. "Heyyyyy! Everybody!"

"My daddy!" Alise said.

"Heyyy!" Fractal said.

"Hi!" Cammy said.

"Here come my mama!"

Mrs. Breckenridge came in. She was as tiny as her

husband was big and broad-shouldered. "Whew! The rain! I'm telling you! Alise, honey, come get these groceries." She stopped short when she saw Cammy and Fractal, looking from one to the other. Suddenly she seemed watchful, careful. "Well! Hello — young ladies!" she said cheerfully. "Let me see. This is — Cammy!"

"Right!" Cammy said, grinning. "And this is Jah-nina —"

"Oh, I know who she is," Mrs. Breckenridge said, looking hard at Fractal.

"She's here from New York-Queens," Cammy couldn't help finishing.

Fractal stood silently. Her face was closed tight. It surprised Cammy, the way she seemed to be holding herself in, away from them.

Knowing their manners, both of them came forward politely, to be embraced by the Breckenridges. Alise, also, was in the greeting circle of hugs.

Cammy thought it nice the way you could always hug the relatives who had come from far.

"Now, I'm right, aren't I?" Mrs. Breckenridge said to Fractal. "You and Cammy —" She paused, to let Fractal speak.

Fractal backed out of the embrace. They all did. She looked at her foot, stubbing at the floor: "Cammy's father's brother's mother's sister's daughter's daughter, 's who I am," she said.

"Whoa!" Mr. Breckenridge said.

Cammy giggled. "She stays with Uncle George, and his wife is Aunt Bessie, and their daughter is GiGi," Cammy said. "She and GiGi are . . . close. And Uncle George's —"

Fractal interrupted her. "I can tell it." Spoken quietly. Her glasses always seemed to shut out everyone. "My mom is the daughter of Clara James, the sister of Uncle George's mom, Tillie. My mom's name is Dayna Madison," Fractal said. "She couldn't come."

"I do remember everybody, when reminded," said Mrs. Breckenridge. She glanced to the side, in an odd way, as though not to look directly at Fractal. But she smiled all around. "Tonight, I'll have Alise write it all out. I don't know all the young families with new babies."

She interrupted herself. "Girls! I bought hot dogs — let's have us some hot dogs! Morris said he wouldn't be along till later."

"I'll set the table," Alise said. "And put the water on."

"Put the water on first," her mama said.

"Yeah, first," Alise said.

With a slight smirk, Fractal stared at Alise an instant.

You shouldn't make fun of people, Cammy thought. *Patty Ann — I was mean, making fun of her.*

That fast, Cammy's drowned cousin was on her

mind. She blinked her back. She felt uncomfortable, and didn't know why, exactly. Fractal acted even odder than before. Mrs. Breckenridge gave Fractal quick side looks when she thought Fractal couldn't see her.

I don't know. Something, Cammy thought. *Funny, going on.*

Politely, she and Fractal agreed to join the Breckenridge family for a hot dog. "We had some food over at Miss Perry's," Cammy said.

"Miss Alice Perry?" Mrs. Breckenridge asked. "Is she still alive?"

"She was when we left," Fractal said coldly, and gave a halfhearted grin so she wouldn't appear a wiseacre.

"She a cousin, too?" Alise asked. "Miss Perry?"

"No," Mr. Breckenridge said. He leaned on a counter where he had put the groceries.

"Well, now, wait a minute," Mrs. Breckenridge said. She thought a moment. Then, gave up. "Cammy, you ask your mama. Know we have some cousins in town," she went on. "You know, you sit down with them in church. But you don't go visit them much. Send a little gift, for marriage." She patted Fractal's arm, leaning close, looking into her face. Fractal sat, rigid. "But you don't think of them as close." Mrs. Breckenridge then patted Cammy's arm.

Fractal and Cammy exchanged looks. Slowly it came to Cammy that, yes, she knew there were relatives other than Aunt Effie's family in town. Miss Perry might be a closer relation, or just maybe like a close family friend. When Alise and her mom conversed, Fractal whispered to Cammy, "You know them, in town?"

"Yeah, I do," Cammy said. "But they aren't what we call close family. Not like real cousins, you know? Not like second or third cousins."

"You don't hang with them, you mean. You weird country people!" Fractal whispered.

Cammy wanted to tell her to shut her face. Tell her that she and her family were not at all "country." What did that mean, anyway? But she didn't whisper another word.

They sat comfortably at the kitchen table as Alise and her mom put the groceries away. Soon, Alise served them fat, spicy hot dogs; the buns, warmed in the oven. Cammy smothered her hot dog in relish. Fractal had ketchup and onions on hers. Mrs. Breckenridge made Kool-Aid. Mr. Breckenridge took his two hot dogs and his newspaper into the dining room. Alise brought him coffee. Then, Mrs. Breckenridge, Alise, Cammy, and Fractal sat, eating together.

"So funny," Alise said. No one had been talking. They looked at her. "Here I am, in somebody's house." She smiled at Cammy, at Fractal. "I don't know him much, but he's a relative, he's Cammy's dad! Here's Cammy and Jahnina! I don't know them, much, either. But we are close, like we all been here all along, huh!" She smiled happily.

Not so dim, Cammy thought. Cammy smiled. They all agreed, with Mrs. Breckenridge leading them, that no matter what kin's house you went to, you always sat down to eat, to "break bread" with the relatives there. Even while smirking, going "heh-heh" all the time, Fractal did agree. That it was a sweet mystery, the way they could be at once close with far relatives.

Cammy could say she liked Alise. She thought of her as kind of sweet. "Cousins," Cammy said. "Alise, are you my first or second?"

Mrs. Breckenridge spoke about it as she got up to get more to drink. "We come out of the Odie's side as well as Uncle Earl's," she said. She put a pitcher of drink on the table and sat down again. "Elodie's mama is my third or fourth cousin. Her mama and I grew up like sisters. But then she went off on her own. There was some kind of squabble, something. And she just had to be going all the time. She ended up picking."

"Picking?" Fractal said.

"Yes, following the crops," Mrs. Breckenridge said. "That's what she likes to do. She picks fruits and vegetables. And you can't change her for nothing!"

That stopped Fractal right in her tracks. Cammy

watched her face. There were things Fractal didn't know about, either. "So that makes Alise Cammy's *fourth* or *fifth* cousin," Fractal said. She gave wide eyes to Cammy over her glasses.

"Something like that," Mrs. Breckenridge said.

Alise's face fell. Cammy was quick to say, "Let's just call everybody second cousins. That's what I do with El, Elodie Odie. Because her mama and my mama are second cousins, which makes El my third cousin."

"Let's call everybody second cousins!" Alise hollered as though she'd just thought of it.

"Oh, goody, let's do!" Fractal said with a tight, crooked smile.

Cammy could have kicked her. Fractal wasn't being nice, she could tell. Because of Alise being dim? Cammy decided to ignore Fractal.

The little boy, Junie, gave out a wail upstairs.

When Alise brought Junie down to the table, he watched everybody. He ate half a hot dog, staring at Cammy and Fractal. *Cute little cousin,* Cammy thought. *Big brown eyes.*

"Can you say 'Cammy'?" Alise asked him.

He wouldn't say anything. He kept chewing and staring and kicking his legs until Alise took hold of his legs and held them still.

"Where is everybody staying?" Cammy thought to ask.

"We're upstairs — GiGi's mom and dad are over

at Effie's — they already moved over there," Mrs. Breckenridge said. "Jahnina," she said to Fractal, "Bessie said to just call if you want to move, and Uncle George will come get you. GiGi said she would move over, and they took her things. It's just for the weekend. Doesn't really matter where anyone stays. We are all relatives!" She laughed nervously. "You can stay here, if you want," Mrs. Breckenridge went on to Fractal. "I know your —"

"— I'm staying here." Swiftly, Fractal cut her off. Glasses glinting, she stared hard at Mrs. Breckenridge. "I mean, I already put my stuff away," Fractal said. Her voice softened. "I didn't bring that much."

"Well, fine, then," Mrs. Breckenridge said. "I told Bessie my family would stay here, in the room that she and the Reverend had. There are extra beds. Alise and Junie can stay in there with us. So Jahnina, you're all right just where you are. It all works out."

Fractal was silent, arms folded tightly across her chest. She wouldn't look at anyone.

"What was that all about?" Cammy asked Fractal later.

"Huh! Trying to boss me around, shoot!" Fractal said. "I wasn't going to move out!" Angrily, "If it was me, though, I sure wouldn't share a bedroom with my folks." Then, with a smirk, "I don't see my dad like you do." In Cammy's face, "And don't ask me about him, too."

Well, I wasn't going to!" Cammy said. She gave up trying to figure Fractal out.

Her dad's house was changing troops, so to speak. But Cammy felt all right with this new arrangement and Fractal, in Fractal's room.

They had left the table, leaving the Breckenridges. "I'll see y'all again. I'm going to hang up my dress for tomorrow," Alise had said. She had her arm around little Junie.

Upstairs, they were behind the closed door in Fractal's room. "Now you get this room all by yourself," Cammy thought to say. "GiGi's crazy to stay over at Aunt Effie's."

"Yeah? Why?" Fractal asked.

"Because Aunt Effie's not all there," Cammy said. "But only I know it, and Andrew and El. Maybe Richie."

"Not even your mom knows it?"

"No?" Cammy said it as if it were a question. "Mom thinks Aunt Effie is getting over Patty Ann's death." She paused, waited. Fractal's eyes were barely there through her tinted lenses. Cammy shook her head. "Aunt Effie's an evil ole space cadet, lost her helmet." She paused. Changed the subject. "And . . . and you ought to know, we didn't drown anybody — me and El. I don't talk about your dad, and you don't talk about what you don't know about." Then, she shut up. She nearly stunned herself, saying all that.

"Okay, Mouse, 'nuff said, for the time being. You only talk about what you know about! Heh-heh!"

"No 'for the time being,' either," Cammy said under her breath.

Fractal heard her. "Yeah. Oh, yeah!" Not looking at Cammy, she took her computer in her arms and marched out of the room. Fractal went down the hall to Morris Coleman's bedroom.

"No, you can't just do that!" Cammy hurried in. "Fractal, don't bother anything! You shouldn't be in here."

"Girl?" Fractal said. "Cool it, I'm not hurting anything." She sat at the desk. Moved Cammy's dad's computer over and put hers next to it. "It's plugged in," she said. "Maybe my plug will reach." She scooted over.

Cammy went into a slow burn; then, out of it again. The only way to stop Fractal was to start a fight — push her, something.

"There. I can reach. His can reach. Sit down, girl . . . Cammy. Here." Fractal pulled up a canvas captain's chair for her.

Reluctantly, Cammy sat down in front of her dad's computer. She didn't feel right, being there. Bedrooms were private.

"Now," Fractal said. "It's prolly got Windows. Windows is an OS, an operating system. First, we have to turn everything on — here — and go in as a guest on his computer. His is connected to a phone line." Shown how, Cammy did it. The machine turned on. It made noises booting up. "Windows-plus 95" came on the screen. "Better than mine!" Fractal said. "I just have Windows 95."

Cammy looked over, saw the difference in the picture.

Colorful little squares spread out on the screen. "You click on the icons," Fractal said, "and they open up the programs you use. With the little icon windows on it, the screen is called the desktop."

"The icon windows. The desktop," Cammy murmured. The whole thing with computers was like a dream to Cammy. She couldn't get used to it as more than a fantasy place, unreal.

"Well, Yiddle Mouse," Fractal said, "the keys won't burn you! Heh-heh."

Gingerly, Cammy put her hands on the keyboard. She was scared her dad would get home, catch her at his computer. *No business doing this!* she thought. But that was the last fear-thought she had.

What was the Internet? She wanted to see it. Was the Mandelbrot Set there? She had to know things. Couldn't help herself.

CHAPTER TEN

Weaving Webs

&

"YOU HAVE to have a screen name, Mouse. We'll use one of mine," Fractal told Cammy, "or you can't get online on the computer to do things.

"Okay," Fractal went on, "if you can type, put in bodeep, and don't capitalize it."

"Bodeep . . . ?" Cammy asked. She could type, but not fast.

"Just do it, Mouse! Spelled, b-o-d-e-e-p."

"I'm doing it!" Carefully, slowly, Cammy did it.

"Now. Take your hands off. I'll put in the password," Fractal said. "You never see the password after the first time you put it in, and you never tell it to anybody."

"'Cause it's so private," Cammy said cautiously.

"It's who you are online. The server recognizes it

and lets you in. You don't want anyone else getting in under your name." Fractal typed, and little stars appeared in the password line. She pressed Enter.

"I'll take you where kids go," Fractal told her. "The Internet is vast. Places you can't go, shouldn't go, and never go. Places that don't allow kids in. Bad places, sometimes. But lots of good places, fun things. There are thousands, maybe millions of Web sites on the Net."

Cammy felt like crying. She took a deep breath. "I don't know what you're talking about!"

"Well, Yiddle Mouse, I'm gonna show you! A Web site is what you call a page. It is a place, an address." Fractal spoke excitedly. "It tells about somebody's line of work, through words and pictures, and if they're selling something."

"Is this the Internet?" Cammy asked.

"We're on my service, which is connected to a collection of other computers. Hit that green icon. Okay. Now we're coming to the Net. I'm typing the address of a place on this link line. Now. We're going to the kids' place. It has to load." After a minute the screen filled. "All kinds of stuff is here, see?"

"'Games,'" Cammy read. "And it says, 'Chat. Make things.'"

"You can get help with math or English stuff. Schoolwork," Fractal said.

"Wow!" Cammy said. "It says, 'Clubs. The Web.'"

"The World Wide Web puts a lot of stuff under

one roof. It makes it easy to get around on the Internet," Fractal told her.

"Where is the Internet?" Cammy wanted to know.

"It's right where we are. It's everywhere — a network, a global connection of computers and people linked by telephone and cables. Don't worry about it, Mouse! Just do it!"

"Okay, I'm doin' it!" Cammy replied. She felt the excitement of discovery. And soon, she was deep into it, starting with kids' stuff. Big kids and little kids and fun places called "sites." Kid zines were magazines for kids of all ages. There was *National Geographic Online* and Nickelodeon Online. Blackberry Creek® was a fun house where you could hang out and write stuff and paint, also.

Cammy was caught in it — cyber space! Suddenly, she was in a place with purple chairs. A clown held up a sign. She knew by now to click on everything that caught her attention. All signs. The sign said, "Dog Here, Dog Gone!" She clicked on it. An animated pink poodle walked to the center of the computer screen and looked at her.

"Oh, wow!" Cammy said.

A white cartoon balloon appeared over the poodle's head. "Hi! What's your name?" appeared in the balloon.

Fractal said, "Put your name in that line there. Then, press 'Enter.'"

Cammy did it and suddenly was in a place of many kinds of dogs, with the animated poodle leading her around. It all happened so fast, Cammy didn't realize she was painlessly learning about beagles and bloodhounds, terriers and collies. Learning which dogs were good with children, which could hunt, which were watchdogs.

"It's for kids who maybe want a dog but don't know what kind," Fractal explained.

Cammy was hardly aware when they left the Internet. Switched machines, even, back to Fractal's machine, which didn't have a phone line to use.

They sat close together now, as Fractal booted up her software, and the magical mystery Mandelbrot Set came on the screen. At once, it sucked Cammy in.

That's the way her dad found them, heads practically together, eyes locked on the computer screen. He slipped into the room unseen by Cammy, although she was aware of someone. But the whole Mandelbrot filled her mind. She and Fractal murmured back and forth. Fractal would lead, and Cammy would follow.

Cammy's dad laughed. He was behind them, looking over their shoulders.

"Dad!" Cammy reached up for him. He put his arms on both their shoulders.

"I've been showing her fractals," Fractal said casually.

"Great!" he said.

Cammy remembered that her dad knew about most things on computers. "I used your computer," she told him, shyly. She hunched her shoulders.

"Well, I guessed you'd want to use mine when you saw hers," he said.

"I showed her the kids' place, stuff like that. Then we did my new software," Fractal said. She talked casually to Morris Coleman.

"Only, Dad?" Cammy began. "It costs a lot. She can only use it another week. Then she has to pay for it." Cautiously, "I figured I could help her pay for it."

"She wants to do fractals with me," Fractal said. "We can e-mail each other about it."

"Dad, she doesn't have the money, and I only got nine dollars."

"Whoa! Slow down, guys," Morris Coleman said. "And you want me to make up the difference?" he said seriously to Cammy. He looked pointedly at Fractal. She kept her eyes on the computer screen.

"Oh, never mind, you don't have to," Fractal said.

"Wait, don't be so quick, Jah. I only want to get it straight," he said.

"Well, I have fifteen dollars," Fractal told him. "She has nine," talking about Cammy. "It costs twenty-nine ninety-five."

"So you need six."

He called her — Jah? Cammy thought.

"Yeah," Fractal was saying.

"But Cammy will need the software, too," Cammy's dad said.

"What?" Cammy said.

"Yeah," Fractal said again, "she will."

Then, understanding, Cammy said, "No, but you don't need to buy me anything!" She was afraid he would get mad at her.

"Well, I can see it's got you hooked, Cammy," he said. He smiled at her. "You didn't even see me come in, you were so deep into it. Look, I can spare six dollars for Jah if you're going to spring for nine. Your reward for being generous is — ta-dahhhh! You can have the software, too!"

Cammy couldn't believe her ears. "Really?" *But, Jah?* she was thinking.

"Cammy, first, you should download the software. Use it for the time they let you," he said. "Jah's program must be shareware. Shareware lets you sample for a certain length of time, to see if you want to buy."

"Sample, fifteen days," Fractal said.

"But, Dad, I don't know how to download stuff. I don't know anything about computers!" Cammy said.

"Cammy, I'll show you," Fractal told her.

"Jah'll show you," her dad said.

Jah? "Jah sounds like a nickname for Jahnina."

He nodded, glancing from Fractal to Cammy. He wasn't smiling.

"I call her Fractal," Cammy said. She giggled. "That's what GiGi calls her. El does, too." El. She'd nearly forgotten about El. Home.

"Okay, is it settled, then?" her dad asked. "Jah, you get my six, Cammy gives you her nine. You help her download the software into my computer. I'll have to put her on my account, too. And after that, we'll see if she's interested." He smiled at Cammy, patting her shoulder.

"I will be," she said.

"She will be," Fractal agreed. "There are some wild fractals all over the Internet."

"Okay. I'm going to get something to eat. Then I've got to go back to close up the place," Morris said. "What are you two up to?"

They shrugged. "Have you been over to the pool yet?" he asked Cammy. He didn't wait for her to answer. "Well, don't ride the bike on the roads after dark. Your mother'll be upset if you do."

"I know," she said. "Maybe we'll stop by the pool on the way back."

He gave them each a pat on the head. "Bye, Dad," Cammy said.

"Maybe I'll see you later," he told her.

"See you later, Daddy," Fractal said.

His right hand on Cammy's shoulder; the left, on Fractal's.

Everything inside Cammy shut off, smothering her. It came back on, racing in her, jagged, sucking at air. *SeeyoulaterDaddy*. There began a whirling ache in her head of odd things said, *Daddy,* strange looks. Bits of cold, *see you* swelled her throat, *Daddy-Daddy* beat in her chest. *Jah. Dad.* Wounded, she held her stomach. Freezing, shivering down her back. *Daddy.* She paled, and went to pieces.

"Cammy." Her dad.

Rising, she pushed back. Knocked into Fractal. Fractal reached for her. Cammy pushed her away. A swirling was in her brain: her mom . . . my mom. . . .

"Cammy!" Her dad caught her arms.

Don't! "Get away!" she told him, elbows out at him and — *Jah!* Shoving them with all her might. Whirling, flailing her arms, she pushed Morris Coleman, her . . . So angry! Inside her, words, pieces: Fractal, age, Andrew and me. When?

Not just *my* big ole dad. She covered her face. And cried. Sobbing.

Pieces. *My* mom. *My* dad. *Her* mom. Her, *the other one*.

"Cammy, don't. Please. I'm sorry." Her dad.

But she was on her way out of the room, embarrassed to death. *I thought you were mine! Why! Get away!*

Her dad caught her. "I don't want you to run away, Cammy. I know it's a shock. But these years — with her so far away, there was no need.

Now Jah's at my brother's. I can see her. She's right with us. You two need to talk. Don't hate me, Cammy."

Cammy sobbed, fighting him, trying to get away. *I hate you!*

"Daddy, this isn't right," Fractal said.

"You be quiet!"

"Let her go, Daddy."

"Shut up, Jah. I know what I'm doing."

"No, you don't!" she said.

"You want me to send you back?" he asked her. "I mean, really send you back!"

Cammy stood. Looked away into the sudden, cruel silence. She dropped her arms. Her big ole dad. Love you, eyes like mine. Wasn't nice anymore. Wasn't hers.

She was facing him. Saw his jacket buttons. He had her by the shoulders. She'd stopped struggling, and he eased his grip on her. "I want you to stay here with Jah just for a while," he said. "I want you both to get to know one another. It sounds hard, I know, but it's got to be this way. I can't help it. Only you two can do it, Cammy."

He bent down, his face close to hers. "Not her mom, not yours, can do it. Jah's wise, and so are you. You are so alike! Don't turn away! That's all I have to say — except, I will never be sorry she's my daughter, too.

"You're to stay here. Listen to me. It's the best

way. Don't run. Jah, keep her here. I'll be down-stairs for a while."

Then, he left. Her dad. Left her in the room with the other one. No two ways about it.

Cammy sucked in air as if her last breath was com-ing. Her face was wet; her nose ran. She didn't know a thought for what she was feeling. But to just leave her here! Close to the bed, she fell on it partway, and slipped to the floor. She lay racked with gasping, on her side. Her hands trembled, touching the bed-spread.

She didn't know when she realized Fractal was next to her. Stretched out on the floor, Fractal leaned over her and dropped a bunch of tissues into her hands.

Long time. Silence. Then, finally, "Hey, Yiddle Mouse?" said softly. Fractal. "Huh. He's wrong, you know? He is dead wrong. Outrageous. Leaving us here. I mean, where's he supposed to be? Huh!" Bitter laugh.

"Look," Fractal went on, "it's what it is, okay? At least you had him here where you could see him. And it's a lie, he cared about me," Fractal said. "If he had, I'd-a got more than a phone call every six, eight months. 'When will I see you, Daddy?'" Mim-icking herself; then, him: "'I'm coming there, I promise, next summer.' Huh! He'd'uv told you about me, 'stead of keeping it from you, if he cared about me. I mean, I almost never saw him until I moved from Detroit to New York."

Cammy stayed still, afraid to say a word, for fear she would cry or stop breathing. She sucked air in gasps she couldn't stop yet. Like a kid. A baby. She was just who she was, that's all. She wasn't smart or big, like . . . *Jah*. And that made her cry more.

"Hey. Hey, come on, Cammy. He should be in this room with us."

"I want to go!" Cammy managed.

"Then go. I won't stop you. But please don't. Don't go for a minute, okay?"

"You're not . . . my friend!" Cammy cried.

"Mouse, listen."

Shouting, "I'm not a mouse! Don't . . . don't you call me that. You . . . you don't know me!"

Sitting up, Fractal kept quiet. Cammy found she was sitting, too. She hadn't realized. Fractal had her glasses off; her eyes were wet. She wiped them with a tissue; then wiped her lenses. Cammy saw Fractal's eyes, like her own. "You . . . cried," she said huskily.

"So what. Think I can't?" Fractal said. "Listen up, I'll tell you something. You'd better not tell anybody! Because if you do, I might get rough! And for sure, I'll never speak to you again."

Cammy thought about it. Finally said, "What?"

"You don't tell," Fractal warned her.

"What?" Cammy could take a deep breath now. She wiped her face and blew her nose. She wasn't going to promise anything.

"I always felt something missing," Fractal said. "Not just my daddy. And after me and GiGi got here? When you walked in the bedroom where GiGi and I were? I knew. 'Cause, for as long ago as I can remember, I wanted a little sister. And when I knew who you were, I got one."

"You're not . . . either," Cammy managed.

"Yes, I am," Fractal said.

"But . . . just half," Cammy said. Her eyes filled.

"Two halves make a whole, don't they, Mouse?" Fractal said gently.

It took Cammy a long time to say something. She heaved a large, ragged sigh. Drew herself in, finally. Stubbornly stared at nothing. "Don't call me Mouse," she said.

CHAPTER ELEVEN

Did Everybody Know?

❧

EL'S MOM, Marie Lewis Odie, had come to Cammy's house in the way early hours of Saturday morning. Came up to wake El first thing.

El pulled her mom in bed with her, wrapped her arms around her. "Been waiting the whole night!" El told her. And fell fast asleep again before her mom could say, "Baby girl, I missed you!"

Cammy came to, slowly. Aunt Marie was singing softly to El.

"I've been hungry, I've been cold, and now, I'm growing old! And the worst will come, it sure always seems. . . .

"Oh, my beans, bacon, and gravy; they nearly drives me crazy. I eat them till I see them in my dreams. . . .

"As I wake up every morning, with another day a-dawning, I know I'll eat another plate of beans!"

Cammy fell asleep listening to the sound. It wasn't sad. It was full of the strength of the singer, whose face was the nicest in the world.

". . . and everyone is happy, so it seems.
"Well, when the pickin' is all done, we straighten up one by one. And thank the Giver for our plate of beans."

Long before Aunt Marie had arrived, Cammy had come home from her dad's. Alone, no pool, no one with her. She'd eaten a sandwich, gone upstairs, and curled up on the bed. When it was dark out, she could hear visitors, relatives, downstairs. Young cousins, who had decided to sleep out in Aunt Effie's yard and in Cammy's. They moved back and forth, up and down the streets, until almost midnight, wrapped in blankets, sheets. Until a cruising cop car stopped, shone the light on them. "You're not from here, are you?" And they explained it, the 'union. And the cops said, "Look, find a home before somebody gets into difficulty." City kids stayed quiet, polite, not knowing if they would be frisked. They would not be, not this time. Everybody knew the Colemans.

All of it, told to Cammy by one Elodie Odie. "Kids, out lookin' for a home!" El had said. She was excited by all the cousins arriving. Happy, with her mom around, visiting. Cammy stayed in her room, watching, sometimes, from her window.

There hadn't been a good chance to catch her own mom, Maylene, until way late. Cammy didn't care. *Just so long as no one sees me,* she thought.

Earlier, Effie had Gram Tut with her, with the visitors, over at her house for a while. Cammy's mom was in and out seeing everybody with Andrew. And relatives came, and her mom brought Gram Tut back.

"Gram loved seeing all the relatives, Aunt 'Lene said," El told.

El hadn't busted in on her. She'd been going in and out of the house, and sometimes she would come upstairs to tell Cammy stuff. Told about the cousins having a fit about the quiet, small-town night.

El was gone again, and Maylene came upstairs.

"Cam." She sat on Cammy's bed and reached to hold her. But Cammy shook her head. "So. El says you heard . . . about . . ."

El's got a big mouth. Cammy stayed quiet.

"Are you angry at me?" Her mom wanted to know. Cammy didn't have to say. Her mom could tell she was holding back. Shock. Resentment.

Finally, Cammy said, "Why didn't you ever say anything? Everybody knew but me!" Afraid she'd cry, she shut up.

"No, not everybody," her mom said. "I . . . didn't want to talk about it, or think about it. I hoped that child would never come here."

Cammy couldn't believe it. She'd always thought her mom and dad were so right. But now, she knew both of them had been wrong. Didn't know how wrong, exactly. She just knew that her mom was hurt by it, and shamed by . . . *Jah*. Her dad was apart from them because of it; and separate from her and her mom, and . . . *Jah*.

"Better not say what *it* is," Fractal had told Cammy before she left for home. "I can think *it*. But if I don't say *it*, *it* can't make me feel bad."

Keeping a kid, a half . . . relative — secret from her, Cammy. Hurting the secret kid and Cammy, too. Mom, splitting from Dad over *it*, she guessed. Everybody hurting, getting hurt, one way or an-other. She didn't want to hear or think about the "more to *it*" that Fractal said she just kept out of sight in her own mind.

"I want to sleep," Cammy told her mom.

"We'll talk later," her mom said, relieved.

Why talk later? Cammy thought after her mom had gone.

But she and El talked, a little.

El came back, came close, looked at Cammy.

Cammy could smell the outdoors, the night on Elodie. Hot out, clear. A night for city kids to scare themselves.

"I'm not asleep," Cammy said.

"Your mom tell you stuff?" El asked.

Cammy shook her head, meaning she didn't want to talk about it.

"Did you know about me . . . Fractal?" Cammy asked finally.

"Nuh-uh, not till GiGi told me. She said not to say anything. She said your dad had to tell you stuff."

Cammy's mouth turned down. Her dad never did.

She didn't cry. She and El didn't talk about anything to the point. El would look away, then look back at her. She'd touch Cammy, pat her arm, and touch her fingers. Measure Cammy's hand with her own. El put her face near Cammy's and rocked back and forward. It was closeness, without saying so; friendship, the way they were before GiGi, and maybe always would be.

"All kinds of stuff happens," Cammy murmured. Eyes closed.

"Good things and bad things," El agreed. "My mom's with me, but she'll go again. I mind it, but it has to be."

"Good and bad can happen to anybody." Cammy pictured a scale, and she weighed everything. "It's done with," Cammy said. Speaking about her half sister, City Mouse.

"You didn't have a thing to do with that," El said.

Fractal didn't, either, Cammy thought. *Her, half to me, and me, half to her. Makes one whole mess.*

Still, by Saturday, when everybody was out and about, Cammy had a hard time figuring how to act. The pull of GiGi on El had stolen El away from Cammy again. El was at GiGi's side now, and with lots of cousins. GiGi taught them some dances.

Cammy was alone, outside, to the edge of her yard and up and down the street for a while. She had her bathing suit on under her shorts. Everybody did. They'd have to swim at some point. But she felt numb all over. City Mouse was nowhere to be seen. She tried being different from herself. She became smiley, giggly. A cousin came up to her. "Hi, you're Cammy. I'm Malika, and Asia's my sister. We're going to ride in Andrew's truck to the park. People are already there."

Cammy felt shy and silly. She barely responded. Tearful, as the girl walked away, she became herself — it was a feeling. And she did not know who she was.

You didn't have to say hello all the time to cousins. She would climb in the truck as they did, on one of Andrew's loads to the park. She didn't bother thinking about where she would be going. Andrew came around to close the truck gate, and she was still standing there on the sidewalk in front of her house. He clamped both hands around Cammy's head. Looked into her face.

"Don't turn your mouth down," he said, so quietly, just to her. "You're all right. Everything's fine. It's no big thing, Cammy."

Big ole Andrew! But she had to say, "Then why was it a secret? You must've . . . why didn't you tell me?"

"That was just Mom's way, and Effie's; made me promise. They're living in retro. They're in retreat from the front. Mom is also stubborn."

Mom! She was always so right! Cammy felt downhearted, exposed.

"Cammy, nobody's staring. Just be yourself."

She gave him a weak grin. Then, Richie was there. "Hey, Cammy!" he said, glad to see her. That made her feel better.

"Richie-mahn," she said jokingly.

"Get in, Cammy," Andrew said. "We'll lift you."

They lifted her by her arms. She could have got in by herself. But she was shaking. "Take it easy, Cam!" Andrew. All the kids, watching now. They made room as she was lifted into the truck bed. But they didn't seem to think she was a freak. Then, Andrew and Richie got in, Richie driving.

It was a nice old ride, with the noon breeze flowing over them. Kids chattering, keeping their voices at medium loud. Talking about the night before and walking barefoot in the streets. Cops. Stars. Never had seen so many stars, some of them said. And the moon! Looking all big!

Cammy found out she didn't have to smile at cousins. One day, she'd recognize them by their first names. It would take her a while to know how they were all related. For the time being, they all called each other "second cousins." She might've suggested that. But everybody was talking at once. Their names went in and out of her memory as they went through town — Malcolm, Teena, Darlene, Malika, Shawna. There were small kids — Asia, Sunanna, and Billy Levi — where was little Junie? Where were the others? El, Alise, GiGi, Fractal-*Jah!*nina.

Kids talking about grass and trees, like they'd not known them before. Houses. Everybody has his own house? No. And just like where we come from? No. Where do you come from? From Ashland. From Cleveland. Memphis. Really? And you lived here all your life, Cammy?

Uh-huh.

You like it?

Uh-huh.

Well, who wouldn't? All this space. You know, have a yard and a backyard. Someday, I will. So will I. Me, too. Shoot. I just like small towns, where you can sit out at night, talk to neighbors.

Some of them joked, laughed off their own small misfortunes. And most of them had just as many problems as Cammy. Maybe more, some of them. Some of them had like El had. Some, not much. Cousins, all. They could feel it running from one of them to the next in the truck. The invisible bond, the unbroken thread. Who knew where it started?

Through the town and out the main street, they turned left. And they were soon on the dangerous, winding road on the way to the park.

"Whooo-wheee!" kids hollered. "What is this road? Cammy!"

Cammy told. The D-bone. Called that by all the town kids. Called the Devil's Backbone by her brother and Richie.

It had an official name. But the D-bone had been just fine for generations of kids.

Tall trees on each side of the narrow two-lane. Shade and dappled light, making light-dark, light-dark, as they went.

Cammy told them to close their eyes. Better to feel the air. Breeze could dry your hair, wet on your neck. Warm, sweet air. She caught a whiff of onion, wetness that was damp earth in running water. Streams.

Then they were off the D-bone and climbing a steep gravel road.

Be careful, Andrew!

Kids screamed, squeezed their eyes shut, and held

on. A sudden coolness woke them up again, wide-eyed. They were in a pine forest. Amazing, tall, dark pines. *"... in the pines, in the pines, where the sun never shines ..."* Malika sang and, smiling, left off. They turned up their faces and sniffed. The pines gave off a strong scent of turpentine.

It was told, how kids planted all the pine trees, at least for the last seventy-five years. You could see the town from within this pine forest.

Gravel changed to smooth, Tarmac pavement, and they were in the Lewin State Park. They saw wood signs with direction arrows. They passed by the old coach road to Cincinnati. A sign for the upper level of the park and one for the lower level shelter.

Andrew's truck carried them along the road to the lower level. Cammy held her breath; then, breathed out. She'd gone to day camp at the lower level, last year. *It is all right. Don't think. Don't think.* She'd stay, eat, and then go back home to the town pool to swim. Maybe everybody'd go with her. She'd be the leader.

Richie parked in the lot. Then, up the sandy path. Kids and grown-ups, everywhere. Relatives: cousins, aunts, uncles, mothers, fathers. They strolled in and out of the shelter. Made of wood and fieldstone, the shelter was open on every side, with six-foot overhangs that kept it shaded and cool inside. Long tables were lined up, head to foot down the single, roomy expanse. Uncle Earl was at the grill. Tin tubs were full of ice and bottles of soft drinks.

"We could smell the hamburgers all the way up here," kids told him, a bunch of them from the truck, rushing Uncle Earl.

Every long table was set with paper plates and forks and spoons and knives. Family members filled glasses. Potato salad, baked beans, hot dogs, and macaroni casseroles were being placed on the tables. Greens. Relatives must've cooked all the way from early morning. There was oh, so much food. Cammy groaned at the smells.

Fathers and mothers were out in the playing area, some playing ball. Some played horseshoes and baseball. But older people were calling everybody now to come, enjoy. "How many of us are there?" someone asked.

"Don't know," an older cousin answered. Cammy didn't know half the names of everybody. "Maybe ninety."

"Maybe a hunnert-fifty."

"We'll soon know," a grown-up said.

Gram Tut sat near Uncle Earl at the head of a table line in the center of the room. Aunt Effie sat with her, arms folded. Cammy was surprised to see Effie wore a flowered print dress, quite nice. Quickly Cammy went to Tut to get a hug.

"Gram, it's here," she said, "the 'union!"

"I know it!" Gram said. Emmet had come, too. "All told!" Her face swelled with smiles.

"Hi, Aunt Effie. I like your dress!" Cammy said politely.

A slight smile. A nod. Effie kept her stony gaze on the out-of-doors.

Cammy thought to plant a kiss on Gram's cheek, but never did. She felt she'd look silly.

She walked around. Fractal seemed to jump out at her. Suddenly there, on the grass, she was surrounded by kids — El and GiGi, others, whose names Cammy couldn't remember right away. There were boys, a cousin Jordan, stretched out, leaning on elbows.

Who's to introduce everybody? she wondered. Fractal and a boy, Akim, were playing the game, Awale. Cammy knew it was an old board game played with colorful cowrie shells. The object was to capture the other player's shells. The group watched, talking and laughing easily as the game proceeded.

GiGi performed from the waist up as she sat, arms swaying, head pecking and rolling. She kept a running rap about Fractal, the game, who they were. Loud. *"Change. S'the happenin' thang. Up. The way you walkin', talkin', change. Up! Jokin' spoken. Word. Doo up!"* Kids laughed, joined in. There were put-downs. *"You, hard ticket. Better hang still. 'Fore you drop it, pick it, pick it, u-u-up!"* Lots of pointing and "Oooh-hoos!"

Five rounds of the board, and Fractal had captured all of Akim's shells in his six troughs. She won the game. She smiled to herself. Gathered up the cowries and put them in a felt bag. "That's it," she said.

"You cheated. But that's cool," Akim said. "I'll beat you next time."

Fractal stayed mellow, but said, "Jive turkey, don't think so!"

"I haven't never seen anybody but my dad beat Fractal at Awale," GiGi said.

"Do you know how to play?" Fractal asked. She was looking directly at Cammy. Everybody was. That quickly, she knew Cammy was there.

"No," Cammy said. Her voice squeaked, like a mouse.

"I'll have to teach you," Fractal said. Gazed right at Cammy. Tinted no-eyes. Everybody else stared from Fractal to Cammy, and back.

Cammy couldn't find out what to say. Couldn't think what to do with Fractal. Couldn't look at anyone. She slunk away.

But Fractal was never far.

CHAPTER TWELVE

Something More

&

THERE, inside her, something nudged at her. But it would slide away.

She wanted to be happy. It was 'union, after all. She'd waited so long for it. Yet she felt miserable with such a sick feeling. Not just because of *Jah*, although that, too. Her hands, her legs, trembling. Maybe she would vomit. She swallowed. She needed to think about something else.

Her dad, next to her at the table. Andrew, next to him. Fractal, on her other side. She wanted to yell, *"Girl!* Jah! *You don't belong with me and my* daddy *dad!"* But she felt crushed, weakened. Some moments, she could hardly breathe. Long tables full of so many people she didn't know. Spilling out the doorways onto the grassy expanses. There was a

Reidel from town who was going on seventeen, and a Joyce and a DeRhonda from Tennessee. She had met cousins all around. The *Jah*, always near.

Where was her mom? And why wasn't she beside her? Her mom gave Cammy up to Morris Coleman and his Jahnina? No, there she was, her mom and Aunt Effie, eating with other mothers, aunts. Aunt Marie Odie, Aunt Bessie. There was Miss Perry, too!

There were so many, getting up and sitting back down. Teen girls, large, like Alise Breckenridge, re-filling their plates from serving pans of potato salad and baked beans. Tanika Turner was there from town. Cammy never knew she was a cousin. How did it all work? Half cousins? Like half sisters? Did everybody call people cousins even when they were not? Because they seemed to fit with you? Boys, too. Andrew and Richie, up and down, bringing more relish, more hot dogs, hamburgers, mustard, and ketchup. Why didn't the moms, the aunts, sit with them? Why did it all seem familiar and yet new and different? She wanted to tell everyone to sit still, please, sit still. Why did she feel left behind? It all made her dizzy.

Gram! She searched the tables. Someone put a piece of chocolate cake before her. Saw Andrew heading onto the grass. He was pushing Gram's wheelchair. Flowers. Gram had a bouquet across her lap. Her mom. Flowers. Aunt Effie. A really nice print dress. And holding flowers, too.

So many people. So much noise all around. Food smells. Laughter. Everyone eating, talking.

Relatives pasted name tags on themselves. Her dad had one for her. What did it say? *It says Cammy.* Fractal, in her ear. She saw a cart of slender bouquets of baby's breath and fern, moss rose. Her dad told her to eat. She had some cake.

Girls, when they finished eating, got up, went out, each picking a bouquet. She leaned against her dad. He had his arm around her. "It's okay, Cammy," he was saying.

She shook her head. "S'not okay." Voice, just scared.

She felt Fractal take hold of her hand. She stayed very still. Watching everything seem to quit. Less talking. Plates, clean. Empty tables. Some silence. Finished eating. Why did her mom and Andrew go away from her?

She stood between Fractal and her dad. "This way." A man's voice.

"Don't I get a bouquet?" she asked. Knew she would not.

"Of course you do," her dad said.

Fractal placed one in her arms and held on to her. Her dad had his arm around her, too.

"Please, just let me go home," she said.

"Cammy. It's not awful. It's not something you should be afraid of."

I know it is. "Why didn't anyone tell me?"

"Cammy. The reunion is always like this. We all go down to the Little River. You needn't fear. It can be upsetting. But it's not awful."

No! That's not all of it. Where's my mom? She couldn't ask that, like some little kid. *But where'd she go?* "Is my mom going down?"

"Yes, of course," he said. "She went with Richie and Aunt Effie and Andrew. They had to get Tut into the truck. Andrew will drive down where the park rangers have a maintenance road."

Oh, no. *The bluety.* In her mind, the Little River swirled with the whirling blue hole, said to be bottomless. And that was where, last summer, her cousin Patty Ann . . . The bluety had almost taken Elodie; would have, if not for Patty Ann.

Cammy gave a groaning sob. She could feel Fractal's arm around her waist. *Jah!* "You said I drowned my cousin, and I never did!"

Cammy broke away from them and started running. But Fractal caught her. "I was dumb, Cammy. I was stupid, and I'm sorry!" She grabbed Cammy and held her until Cammy rested against her, crying.

Their dad came up. "Jah, you didn't say that!"

"I was being stupid. I told her I was sorry. Hey, Mouse? I apologize. Here, you can hit me."

"No! I don't hit people," Cammy said. *But I do push!*

"Good for you," her dad said.

"This whole thing is stupid, Daddy," Fractal told him.

"Yours is not to reason why," he told her.

"Ours is just to do or die," she said back. But she looked at Cammy. "It's a ceremony," she said. "I've never seen it, either."

She held Cammy by the arm. Cammy let her. Now and then, she looked up at Fractal as they walked with their father across an expanse of grass. Where trees and bushes began, they would go down to the Little River.

They walked directly to a dangerous, slanting hillside. Cammy stopped dead in her tracks. The place had been full of soggy dirt and mud, screaming daycamp kids here a year ago. They had slipped and slid down to a hugely swollen river below.

But now all was dry and graded gradually with wide wood steps cut into the hillside. "It's changed," Cammy exclaimed.

"It's safe now," her dad said. "And they've posted signs about the danger when the rains come."

The steps felt solid under her feet. Her dad went first, with their bouquets under his arm. She and Fractal followed, holding hands. She held tight. Dry bushes, all around.

Halfway down, Cammy heard the river. Something swooshed through her, like ice, melting, running. Would she drown? Her turn?

She could see some of the cousins when there was an opening through thickets. Everywhere, relatives moved along the Little River bank. Now Cammy could hear a smooth, spilling, gurgling. Not hurrying. It was a river you could stand beside and look at. She could see it.

"Well, it doesn't look so tough," Fractal said.

Cammy clung to Fractal with both hands. Waves of fear, anger, sadness flowed through her.

Fractal grinned down at her. "It looks little. That's why it's called the Little River!"

It wasn't little once. "It was flooded up the hillside," Cammy whispered. "It was all wet and slippery out here. El's shoe hit the water. El grabbed at it and fell. There weren't any steps then. There was nowhere to stand or walk, the water was so high up the hillside."

"Okay, Cammy. It's over. It's all right." Her dad. He handed her a bouquet. Gave one to Fractal.

They were standing on wood railroad ties made into a platform. Steps down to the water. It looked as if a bridge was starting to be built over the river.

A rope safety line extended lengthwise about three feet into the water. There, the bank dipped down under the river, getting deeper. Now, girls and boys were wading out in their bathing suits to the rope. Girls held their bouquets high and reached for the rope. Held on.

* * *

Cammy was cooling off; she was in water up to her waist.

All the grown-ups lined the bank by families. Gram Tut was there before them in her wheelchair. Effie and Maylene were on either side of her. All three held their bouquets. The odor of flowers was sweet on the still, warm air.

Tut called out in her reed-thin voice, "TELL!" And the ceremony began.

Families' names were called. They stood together; told who they were. Uncle George started telling, "Come from New York-Queens. I am George Coleman; my half brother is Morris; our father was Taylor Coleman. He married Lorraine, Morris's mother. Lorraine, deceased. Taylor then married my mother, Tillie James. My wife, Bessie Sims Coleman. Daughter is GiGi."

Cammy's dad took it up. "I'm Morris Coleman. My wife is Maylene Wright Coleman. Have a son, Andrew. Two daughters, half sisters, Cammy, daughter of Maylene, and *Jah!* Jahnina, whose mother is Dayna Madison. Dayna is the daughter of Tillie James's sister, Clara. Clara is George Coleman's sister-in-law. But was no relation to me." His mouth in a straight line, steel eyes looking out over the water. And stood still in the huge silence along the gentle river.

All along the rope line, the girls and boys were at

least knee-deep in the Little River. Sometimes they would scrunch down, she and Fractal, and the rest. They floated their bouquets on the water. "We'll be cold out here soon," Fractal said. "Cammy, let everything go. Like the water, touching you and going on. Let it wash around you. Let it go through your fingers."

I can. "I did," Cammy thought to say. And then: "Did my mom want us to be together today?"

"She agreed to it with . . . Daddy."

Above, on the riverbank, one family telling took a while. Her mom let Aunt Effie tell. It seemed all would tell something. Aunt Effie, with tears in her eyes: "Oldest daughter of Tutwilla Duersen Wright, called Tut, and Emmet Wright. Older sister to Maylene Wright Coleman. My husband is Earl Harding. My son is Richard, called Richie. And my dear daughter, Patricia Ann, called Patty Ann by all and sundry — is deceased! Dead, right here in that blue hole!"

Gram Tut, speaking: "All the family, heave your flowers. Our gift to that one, gone. Told."

And they did that, Maylene, Effie, Tut, Cammy, Fractal, GiGi, and Elodie. As part of the family, El's mom told: "I am Marie Lewis Odie. My daughter with me, Eloise, called Elodie. I have sons, not here. Second cousin to Maylene and Effie; first cousin to Tutwilla's Emmet. His brother was my father. These flowers, for the child, gone, and my husband, Vernon Odie, gone." They heaved their flowers out on the water.

A ring of bouquets caught a swirling current moving ever closer to that dark bluety, far out toward the bank across from them. Spiraling, the flowers flowed together. Made a grand crown of colors. Ever more swiftly circling. Until, at last, the crown sank with a sucking, hissing, out of sight.

Gram told. Cammy listened, watching moving water, moving people, flowers, the bluety. All the day awhirl in her head. Arms akimbo, Gram was all there, all herself.

Young ones got out of the water, pulling on shorts, trousers. Some lay on the bank in the sun. Cammy scooted over to Gram's chair and leaned against it. Fractal, not far from her. Her mom, next to her. Cammy felt the sun, hot on her closed eyelids. Inside her, there was dark. Through it came Gram's telling — a light-stream of pictures on the black of Cammy's night:

"TOLD, Long time gone. Passel of folks, moving. Union. Soldiers, ragged, hungry, never left them. Union settled with some of the passel. Some their descendants still live here. They'd crossed the great water, and then they came to this crick. Well, yes, this crick was like a thorn in the side. Swollen River. Like last August.

"Soldiers knew about fighting wars. Knew to be

helpful. Tired, they wanted to settle down. They knew danger would be with them. But that hole — whoosh! They got drowneded.

"In every season. They, some of them, moving on up to better themselves and be safe. They got caught by this crick and never got out. My own grandmother, Callie Cloud. Part native, she was — Cloud. Patawatami.

"Everybody, talking about this family's 'union. Reunion's what it is, and part of the other kind . . . Union. All such words weave around us, hold us in their silk and seams.

"Union, reunion, mean to draw past and present around us. The past keeps on in the cousins. Present is but what will come to pass. River is history, flowing. Like holding to a rope line of time, you are its memory. These flowers for Callie, for all the gone. Lest we forget."

Tut went quiet — a full minute, Fractal said later. Cammy thought it had lasted like a dream.

Tut, listening. Emmet: *Better had take the time to go with me.* She grunted. Searched her hands in silence. Tut: *I'll let you know.* Emmet: *You been here long enough. This, your last 'union.* Tut: *Don't tell me — go back where you came from.* Emmet: *I'm telling you true, Tutwilla.* Tut: *I'll go when I'm ready.*

CHAPTER THIRTEEN

Change

❧

SHE REMEMBERED having a headache. Her dad had given her cold water, and she drank it too fast. Remembered going back up the wood steps in the hillside. It seemed like they were in a parade up from the Little River and crossing the expanse of the park lawn. There were so many people, relatives, cousins. Kids, hurrying to go to the pool. The shelter, emptying out now. A few remaining adult cousins, cleaning everything and making sure the trash was tied up.

Cars, pups — pickup trucks taking kids to the pool. Fractal said the 'union rented the pool for a few hours.

And how come Fractal always knew everything? But the pool, just for them!

Andrew, Richie, and her dad would see that all the kids got in. Aunt Bessie and Uncle George took Gram Tut back home. Kids in the pups returned through town and went on to Vaughn Park Pool.

She was tired. Didn't remember eating. She must've said it out loud.

"You ate," Fractal said. Always near her.

Cammy disliked the city mouse, yet liked her — Fractal, teacher. Her feelings confused her.

They got to the pool, and all of them piled out. They were told there would be towels in her dad's heavy-duty truck. In a minute, he was there, pulling up behind Andrew's pickup. Cammy saw her mom in the truck, and Aunt Effie, like a chaperone. The two of them and her dad, looking through the windshield at them. Her mom sat in the middle, next to her dad.

"Well," Fractal said. Behind Cammy, always near.

Well, nothing, Cammy thought. Her mom and dad. No, and no two ways about it. They wouldn't connect. Nothing would change.

"Well," Fractal said again. "We don't have enough clues to make an intelligent guess."

Just shut your face.

"Here." Fractal unpinned Cammy's name tag. "Why don't people use safety pins instead of straight pins? It scratched you."

Cammy looked up at her. "Why do you wear glasses?"

Fractal grinned down at her. "That's not what you mean."

"Why do you hide behind your glasses, then?"

Fractal was quiet. She gave Cammy a smirk. "We *are* alike! Smart mouth!"

Best not to answer. Cammy kept her smart mouth shut.

Stuff was going on inside Cammy. She didn't want to swim because her stomach felt sick. There was a dull aching, too, on one side of her head. Her mom said once that you could get sick from too much sun. Her face felt burnt, being out by the Little River for so long. Maybe she'd have a sunstroke — heatstroke? She couldn't remember what it was called. Maybe she would die. Maybe she should go on back home with her mom. But she didn't. She stayed.

Her dad made sure everything was all right. Richie and Andrew were there to watch over them as a family. There was one lifeguard. All the rules were in effect; an announcement was made over the PA before they could get in. All the don'ts: Don't run around the pool. Don't take a running jump into the water. Stay out of the deep end if you can't swim. Don't horseplay. Don't throw objects in the pool unless you have permission. Don't make unnecessary noise. On and on.

"Dag," GiGi said. "What *can* we do?"

"You can dive for this," Richie said. He had a red

ball about two inches around. "You can easily see it on the bottom. Dive for it!" He threw it mid-pool.

The big kids and the brave smaller ones who could swim were in the water in a flash and diving. Fractal beat them all, diving smoothly from poolside. She didn't come up with it, though. Two kids both had hold of it — Elodie! And a smaller boy. They tried to get it away from each other.

It looked like fun. "Take it easy," Andrew told them. "Nobody's supposed to get hurt." Cammy watched from the shallow end, sitting on the side of the pool with her feet in the water.

The game went on for a while, until some of the bigger ones got tired of it. Fractal strode to the high board. "No!" escaped from Cammy.

"Oh, yeah!" Fractal said. She hadn't even turned. *Had hearing like ... like a fox!* Cammy thought. Pictured the sleek, red fox she and Elodie had seen once, driving the country roads with Andrew in his truck. *Or maybe she just guessed I'd say that.*

Fractal climbed up. Without a pause, she did a swan dive into the water. Then, all the others who were brave climbed the board.

The lifeguard watched closely. He relaxed after everybody had taken a turn. Richie stood beside the ladder, looking up. Andrew was near, treading in the deep end. Elodie stood next to Richie, shaking her head.

"I'm too scared!" she cried. She kept saying it

until soon everybody was urging her to dive off the high board. They'd seen that she could swim okay. Seen her do a flip from the low board. She cringed, she clutched herself. She was a scaredy-cat until she had everybody practically begging her. Until she was famous.

Cammy grinned.

"I'll come up the ladder behind you," GiGi told El. "Don't be scared. You won't fall."

"Ohhhh!" Elodie said. "Oooooh. I'll hit the bottom."

"You'll hit the water hard if you don't go in right!" someone said.

"Don't do a belly-smacker."

"I won't," El moaned. "Oh, I know I will."

After more begging and more fame, El held her nose and jumped. But she did okay. Hit the water with a *wump*! And a great splash. Everybody applauded. *El, the star,* thought Cammy.

The sun had gone over far to the west, glowing beyond Sunberry. Cammy could feel it on her shoulders. *I'm sick.* As her stomach came up, she got to her feet fast. Ran to the bathroom with her hand over her mouth.

Fractal found her at the sink, washing her mouth out. Breathing in short breaths. Heat was coming out of her temples with the pounding.

"You don't look so good," Fractal said. She felt Cammy's forehead. "I'll get Andrew," she said.

In a minute she came back and led Cammy out to the front, where Andrew was waiting. "Cam?" He put his arm around her. "It's been a long day." All Cammy could do was nod. "I'll take you home. It's about over anyway."

She went with Andrew. She was surprised that when she got to the car, Fractal had followed. She had pulled on her shorts and wrapped her towel around her. She got in next to Cammy. She leaned close to her, said, "You'll be okay."

They rode in silence until Andrew asked Fractal, "Did you enjoy being here? Over at Dad's?" He smiled at her.

"Yeah. It was fun. You have a lot of relatives," she said politely.

"Now you do, too," Andrew told her. And they were silent. No smirks anywhere.

Home, Fractal wouldn't come in, although Cammy's mom was at the door and held it open. Fractal gave Cammy a wave, said, "Later." And then she went back to the pool with Andrew.

"She looks feverish," Effie said, about Cammy. All Cammy wanted was to go to bed.

"Let me give you some soup," her mom said. "Andrew said you were sick at the pool?"

Cammy nodded. "I was," she said, and then, "I don't want any soup." She climbed the stairs. "I can go by myself," she told them. "I'm just worn out."

They watched her go up, but neither Effie nor her

mom followed. Leaving her alone. *Thanks,* she thought, as she crawled into bed.

She could feel shivers all over her. She was too tired to think. But every time she closed her eyes, she saw the river and felt her stomach try to rise. *The bluety. All so many people. Heard tells.* She had to keep her eyes open until, when she closed them, the river, the sounds, disappeared in the park greenery, and so did other memories. She went into a long sleep-time. She woke up in the night and sipped some water. When morning came, she opened her eyes, and all was quiet.

The first thing she felt was how rested her legs and arms were. She woke up, but she didn't open her eyes. She knew the sun was up. Then more sleep. And when she was finally wide-awake, she looked at the clock. "Wow! Ten o'clock?"

She looked for Elodie, but Elodie's bed hadn't been slept in. "Over with GiGi. Well, good," she murmured. Somehow it was okay, this time, that Elodie had left her.

She walked across the room and felt starved when she saw a glass of milk on her desk. *Mom?* But it wasn't her mom who had left it. It was Effie. And in a while, Effie came in. By that time, Cammy had drunk all the milk.

"Maylene is seeing folks off. So I made breakfast for Mom Tut. You want anything, Cam? I made some pancakes."

It took Cammy a minute to answer. She stared. It was as if Aunt Effie were all new. She had on a sleeveless blouse and . . . slacks! "You look nice," Cammy managed, her eyes wide.

"Thank you. Feel good today. Seeing everybody, the 'union. Feels like a new year." She seemed calm. Peaceful.

"Happy New Year!" Cammy told her. And Effie laughed. The first time Cammy could recall her doing that.

Effie even brought pancakes up to her. They were drenched in syrup. "You didn't have to do that!" Cammy exclaimed. "Oooh, they smell good!" Effie had brought orange juice, a napkin, and silverware on a little tray.

"Well," she said. "Why not? You been sick. Better just rest a while. It was something, wasn't it? All the relatives."

Cammy watched her. Hard to believe her aunt was talking to her. Cammy was quick to go along, be a part of this new woman, Aunt Effie.

"I never knew the 'union was going to be busy with so much stuff," Cammy said. "I mean, Aunt Effie? I didn't want to go down . . ."

"I know. The blue hole. Me either, Cammy." Effie was still. Her face, her eyes, turned dark. But she didn't look around the room, the way she usually did. She held her hands together before her; kept herself right there with Cammy, sane for once.

"We gave our gifts. The flowers, our love. All we could give . . . to them."

"Every time, the 'union's going to be like that? When will the next one be?" Cammy asked her. She'd started eating the delicious pancakes.

"Maybe five or six years," Effie told her. "That's soon enough. Hard for all of us to get together in one place. But when we do, it's a renewal. We'll all go down there again, to the river."

Aunt Effie was about to leave when Cammy said, "What about my dad — do you know? My mom?"

"What about them?"

Cammy looked down. Couldn't say: When will they get back together? Will they ever? Didn't dare wish. But Effie knew.

"For some, over time is a healing power," she said. "They see one another."

Cammy stopped chewing. "What?"

"You heard me. You kids think you know everything." Spoken as a fact and not with malice.

"You mean —?" Cammy began.

"I mean, a movie, now and then. A walk, a ride around, talking, a card game with friends, once in a while. Over time, ice water will warm. Um-hum, and there's much under the bridge that's still and deep." Effie folded her arms over her chest. Leaned back on her feet. "It's enough that Maylene had his other child in her house, with you there, and gave that girl supper, too, and the rest of them. All without throwing something upside his head."

Cammy sat very still, staring at Aunt Effie. *How could it be?* "I . . . I didn't know that," she said.

"Well, you didn't need to. It's not your business, Cam. Leave them be. Love what you have, and be glad you have them both."

Cammy nodded, thinking about that.

Aunt Effie left, then. Cammy sat, couldn't tell if she was happy or not. Was this what it was like to get told grown-up stuff you never knew before? You didn't know how you felt? Maybe wished you hadn't even asked? What did it really mean, "They see one another"?

Slowly, she finished eating. When she used her napkin, she found an envelope. It said on the front, "For Cammy."

"What?" Cammy tore it open. There were three things. First, a cutout heart from Alise. "Hey, Cammy, my cousin. Your dad given me your address. Here's mine. So long! We had fun. I love you. Your cousin, Alise." And she had written her address.

There was also a note from GiGi. It said, "Get well soon! From your cousin, GiGi Coleman. I love you!"

Clipped to the note was a card. It had a printed picture of the pear-man! All black, with sparkling outlines. "Nooo!" Cammy cried. "They've gone?" The note had printed on it: *Jah Madison (Fractal).*

Then, bodeep@aol.com. At the bottom of the note was a message to Cammy: "Mouse (I mean, Cammy), the bodeep thing is my e-mail address."

"But I don't know how!" Cammy wailed.

As if reading her mind, the note said, "You'll learn how. I talked to Daddy (get used to it — there's enuf him for us both) and he's going to show you how to get me, and how to get your own password. He gave me the money from you. (We'll get him a present!) Few weeks, we'll both have the software, so practice the computer. He'll leave his book out for you and give you lessons. You'll have to go over to see him all the time. Mouse, sorry you got sick. Too much at once. Sorry to spring me on you like that (smile). Hey, take care. I had a great time 'wit' you. Don't forget me! Your BIG sis, Fractal."

Things just kept moving.

Her mom found her sniffling. She'd cried about having missed Fractal and everybody. "Why didn't you wake me!"

"I keep doing the wrong things, don't I?" her mom said. She looked tired, and sad. She and Cammy hugged.

"Mom." Cammy buried her face in her mom's neck. "S'all right."

She sat up. "Mom, I have to know. Mom. You see Dad, sometimes?"

Her mom looked startled, touched her throat. Nodded.

"Why did you keep that from me?" She felt like crying.

"Cammy." Her mom paused. "Many reasons, I guess. You were busy being a child. There was too much to tell. It wasn't for you to know about. And then, Patty Ann. And Elodie came to live with us." Maylene put her arms around Cammy. "I didn't want to start in on your dad."

Cammy sighed. "And Fractal?"

"But let me tell you something," Maylene said earnestly. "She wasn't the cause of us. . . . We were together long enough for Andrew, for you. We would part, come back. And part again. We were together when you were born. But I didn't like his ways. He liked to go off by himself, a moody man. You and Fractal are about the same age."

"But she said she was thirteen going on fourteen."

"She's maybe a little older than you, but no thirteen, not yet."

Well that city-dittie! Mouse! Hah! Cammy thought.

"She told you she was older maybe because she's smart and ahead of her grade," her mom told her. "Kids never want to be different, even when they are, like Fractal. She's torn. And hurt."

That's why she gets mean in no time, Cammy thought. "He hurt us both," Cammy said. "I'm mad at him. When she called him 'Daddy,' I went b'listic."

"He told me."

"But he wouldn't talk to us. He left us by ourselves."

"He thinks the way he says something is the way it has to be," Maylene told her.

"But it's not," Cammy said. "Fractal said he was wrong, and he got mad at her."

"Well. He sure isn't perfect. Neither am I. I couldn't forgive him for . . ." Maylene looked down at her lap. Her eyes filled, but she didn't cry. She quickly blinked tears away. "Having another child. It was a long time ago."

"With . . . ," Cammy said. "Mom? Say it. Tell me! Please! Having another child — with? It *is* my business. Aunt Effie says it's not. But it is!"

"If knowing makes it easier," Maylene whispered. She sighed deeply. "Having another child, *with* someone else."

"And you guys were married?"

"Separated — not getting along."

"Oh," Cammy said. She had to think about that. But not now. "My head hurts."

They sat a while, and Maylene gently rubbed her temples. Cammy didn't ask any more questions. She let thoughts glide in and out of her mind. Swell, that Fractal wrote her good-bye. *We're going to e-mail. I have a big sister.* Thoughts about Elodie. *We have to start getting ready for middle school.*

Gram Tut. Cammy jumped. "Where's Gram?"

"Downstairs."

"Is she all right?" Cammy was halfway out of the room.

"She's fine," Maylene told her. "Here, I'll come, too. Cammy. Wait."

Cammy looked expectantly at her mom.

"I want you to know. There's a lot of good in your father. He's just . . . different. Inside himself somewhere and unable, or unwilling, to get out. Some men are like that. But he loves you. And Fractal. He's proud of you both."

That made Cammy glad. "Fractal says there's enough of him to go around."

Her mom didn't say anything. She nodded.

Downstairs, Tut was sitting up comfortably in her bed, watching television. "Will you turn that thing off?" she asked as Cammy came in. "Either they do the dumbest nonsense, Lordy! Or they talk you to death. Then, they go and shoot each other."

Cammy took up the clicker and turned off the TV. "Watch me, I'm your picture." Cammy danced around à la GiGi. Gram laughed and hugged Cammy onto the bed next to her. Maylene came in on the other side.

"You're the sandwich food, Gram," Cammy told her. "And Mom and me are the bread. Hee-eee!"

Gram laughed and laughed, like that was the

funniest thing. They let her slide her bony fingers through their hair. "My babies. How'd I get two baby girls?" she asked.

"One's mine," Maylene said.

"Oh, that's right. I do have two, though."

"Yes."

"Gram? The 'union is over," Cammy said. "Everybody's gone back home."

"No kiddin'. Well, I know I'm worn out. But over? No, Union will always be there." Her eyes roamed the wall until she found her picture of Emmet.

Now why won't Emmet come inside? It's going to rain hard. Look how gray the crick is. And him, out there, spearin' catfish! Well, that fish do taste! Emmet? Come on in now!

Cammy could tell that Gram had gone off some-where. Maylene patted her mom, soothingly. It brought Gram back.

"Like that river will be always there," Tut contin-ued. "You know, it flows with all-us inside it and in our memories inside us? Yes, indeed. As we know one another, we know it gathers us in. There's no difference between us living, and not. It's good. Union."

She melted back into her pillow. Tired out, her eyes closed.

Speaking to Emmet: *I'm so down and weak to my soul, I think it must be near my peace.*

Emmet: Naw, now, take your time. You got a ways, yet. Cook these fishes first.

How many did you get?

A foot one. Some less than a foot one. One, about ten inches.

Oh, Emmet! She was pleased. She told him, *After I cook them, then.*

Best of all was the way he sat right there on his stool, and watched every move she made at the stove. She waited. Finally, he said it.

Tutwilla, m'love, you are some kind of cooker, you are!

There was a smile on Gram's face before Cammy and Maylene went out, to let her get her rest. They mouthed words. Maylene cautioned, pressing her finger on her lips. But Cammy wouldn't talk. She tried to curl up closer to Gram, but really, she could tell she was getting too big to lie comfortably for long on the hospital bed. So she got up, sat there in the chair. Leaning forward, she peered at her Gram. Saw into her, she imagined. All that was inside she saw as slow and steady, golden, like sun-bright on the water. She watched Gram closely. Maylene watched Cammy's face.

Everything means so much, Cammy thought. *Old age means going, going, like the river flows. And me, I'm twelve, and growing, growing up, like the river, after a hard rain.*

She took a deep breath. Everything seemed too

big and foggy. She had a time getting through to how she felt. She didn't want to be sad. She looked at Gram and knew she'd always love her. But something in her was pulling away, it felt like, from Gram, from everybody, maybe. She didn't know, but she thought she might be out of sorts with her before-'union self. Sort of the way Fractal acted. And she knew all of a sudden how that felt: good and bad. Mean and nice. As if she just might say anything that came to mind. Get frantic in a minute and turn on someone.

She was surprised when she found her mom had slipped away. *Enough,* she thought.

She left the room. Went upstairs. Found a dry bathing suit; shorts and T-shirt. Summer uniform. She took everything she needed to the bathroom and got in the shower. Still thinking, she liked the water hot, even in summer. Stretching her leg muscles, to see if all the soreness had gone — it had. Suddenly she had an outrageous thought. "Come, crazy, out the side of my brain! Brainiac, me! Ohhhhh!" And giggled. And laughed uproariously.

"What. Cammy? It's me."

"Who . . . ? Elodie? Girl, you didn't knock."

"Yeah, I did. But you didn't lock the door, too."

"So? I don't have to. It was closed!" But she didn't mind El. They shared everything, the bathroom included. "El, I've got it — ooh-ooh!"

"Well, I'm bummed," Elodie said. "I had to say good-bye to everybody. You know, Alise said I was her little sister? And hugged me real hard. Wasn't that nice?"

"Yeah, sure. I'm sorry I missed everybody. But El, listen."

"What."

"I've got it."

"You got a game for today?"

"No! Listen."

"I'm trying to. But everybody had to go leave!"

"Listen." Cammy was smiling, holding in her excitement as she washed her hair, her back. Got soap in her eyes; washed it out.

"What do you think about — Christmas — in New York!"

There was a long silence, then: "Oh, my — ohhhh, Cammy!"

"I mean, it'd be coo-el, right?"

"Dag," El said.

"Gad," Cammy shot back. They hooted.

"I'll show you my note from The Girls from New York — let's call 'em that."

"The Girls. The Girls? They're cousins."

"Yeah, but to us, our secret. They're The Girls," Cammy explained. "We'll tell everybody in middle school, 'We might spend Christmas with The Girls from New York.'"

They stared at one another. "It'll never happen,"

Elodie said. But there was a dreamy look on her face.

"Fractal's my sister. I can visit my sister, can't I?"

"Yeah! And GiGi," Elodie added.

"The Girls!" Cammy said, laughing. "You just wait. Me. Fractal. We can think up a lot of stuff to make it happen!"

They spent the day acting their age. They missed the cousins, but they walked downtown anyway, to get ice cream. They acted older, which they were. They got soft ice cream in cones. They strolled by the movie house. It was Sunday and quiet downtown.

Some boys. They longed to talk to them. And wondered out loud, would they see the boys in middle school?

They didn't hang out with anybody. But they hung around the stores. They slurped their cones and watched themselves move in the store windows. Saw their reflections touch their hair.

"Getting hot again," Cammy said. They would go to the pool later. "The ice cream is sweetest and coldest of anything," Cammy said.

"Word."

They didn't hurry home.